Montana
★ MAVERICKS

Welcome to Montana—the home of bold men
and daring women, where more than fifty tales
of passion, adventure and intrigue unfold
beneath the Big Sky. Don't miss a single one!

AVAILABLE FEBRUARY 2009
1) *Rogue Stallion* by Diana Palmer
2) *The Widow and the Rodeo Man* by Jackie Merritt
3) *Sleeping with the Enemy* by Myrna Temte
4) *The Once and Future Wife* by Laurie Paige
5) *The Rancher Takes a Wife* by Jackie Merritt
6) *Outlaw Lovers* by Pat Warren
7) *Way of the Wolf* by Rebecca Daniels

AVAILABLE APRIL 2009
8) *The Law Is No Lady* by Helen R. Myers
9) *Father Found* by Laurie Paige
10) *Baby Wanted* by Cathie Linz
11) *Man with a Past* by Celeste Hamilton
12) *Cowboy Cop* by Rachel Lee
13) *Letter to a Lonesome Cowboy* by Jackie Merritt

AVAILABLE MAY 2009
14) *Wife Most Wanted* by Joan Elliott Pickart
15) *A Father's Vow* by Myrna Temte
16) *A Hero's Hom*
17) *Cinderella's Big Sky*
18) *A Monta*
by Susan Mall
19) *A Family Hom*

D0816122

AVAILABLE JUNE 2009

20) *The Kincaid Bride* by Jackie Merritt
21) *Lone Stallion's Lady* by Lisa Jackson
22) *Cheyenne Bride* by Laurie Paige
23) *You Belong to Me* by Jennifer Greene
24) *The Marriage Bargain* by Victoria Pade
25) *Big Sky Lawman* by Marilyn Pappano
26) *The Baby Quest* by Pat Warren

AVAILABLE JULY 2009

27) *It Happened One Wedding Night* by Karen Hughes
28) *The Birth Mother* by Pamela Toth
29) *Rich, Rugged...Ruthless* by Jennifer Mikels
30) *The Magnificent Seven* by Cheryl St.John
31) *Outlaw Marriage* by Laurie Paige
32) *Nighthawk's Child* by Linda Turner

AVAILABLE AUGUST 2009

33) *The Marriage Maker* by Christie Ridgway
34) *And the Winner...Weds!* by Robin Wells
35) *Just Pretending* by Myrna Mackenzie
36) *Storming Whitehorn* by Christine Scott
37) *The Gunslinger's Bride* by Cheryl St.John
38) *Whitefeather's Woman* by Deborah Hale
39) *A Convenient Wife* by Carolyn Davidson

AVAILABLE SEPTEMBER 2009

40) *Christmas in Whitehorn* by Susan Mallery
41) *In Love with Her Boss* by Christie Ridgway
42) *Marked for Marriage* by Jackie Merritt
43) *Her Montana Man* by Laurie Paige
44) *Big Sky Cowboy* by Jennifer Mikels
45) *Montana Lawman* by Allison Leigh

AVAILABLE OCTOBER 2009

46) *Moon Over Montana* by Jackie Merritt
47) *Marry Me...Again* by Cheryl St.John
48) *Big Sky Baby* by Judy Duarte
49) *The Rancher's Daughter* by Jodi O'Donnell
50) *Her Montana Millionaire* by Crystal Green
51) *Sweet Talk* by Jackie Merritt

Montana
★ MAVERICKS

LAURIE PAIGE
Outlaw Marriage

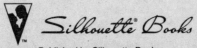
Silhouette Books

Published by Silhouette Books

America's Publisher of Contemporary Romance

Special thanks and acknowledgment to Laurie Paige
for her contribution to the Montana Mavericks series.

SILHOUETTE BOOKS

Recycling programs
for this product may
not exist in your area.

ISBN-13: 978-0-373-31053-1

OUTLAW MARRIAGE

Visit Silhouette Books at www.eHarlequin.com

Printed in U.S.A.

LAURIE PAIGE

says, "One of the nicest things about writing romances is researching locales, careers and ideas. In the interest of authenticity, most writers will try anything… once. I've interviewed fighter pilots, FBI agents and detectives. It's fun to investigate a burglary scene, ride a canoe through white-water rapids or climb on a glacier. Landing on a crystal-clear mountain lake in Alaska in a pontoon plane is exciting. I've ridden a horse, a cow, a donkey, a camel and a pig. But never will I hang glide."

In addition to the above, she's been a NASA engineer, a past president of the Romance Writers of America (twice!), a mother and a grandmother (twice, also!). She was a Romance Writers of America RITA® Award finalist two times for Best Traditional Romance and has won awards from *Romantic Times BOOKreviews* for best Silhouette Special Edition and Best Silhouette novel. She has also been presented with *Affaire de Coeur*'s Reader's Choice Silver Pen Award for Favorite Contemporary Author.

Resettled in Northern California, Laurie is looking forward to staying in one place and eager to experience whatever adventures her next novel will bring.

One

Hope Baxter exhaled a pensive sigh, her gaze on the mountains to the west of Whitehorn. Today the lofty peaks didn't comfort her troubled spirit. Neither did they gain her any perspective on the problems confronting her.

Not that the problems were personal, she hastened to assure herself.

The elaborately hand-carved sign on the lawn that proclaimed the building to be the new headquarters of the Baxter Development Corporation reminded her of her duties. She squared her shoulders and glanced toward the neatly arranged papers on her desk.

As the chief attorney on the case of *Baxter versus Kincaid et al,* she had to be cool, decisive and firm in the meeting with Collin Kincaid. She wondered where he was. Punctual in their prior meetings, he was ten minutes late for this one and he was the one who had requested it.

A movement caught her eye. She paused, her attention on the street in front of the building, and watched as a tall, agile rancher climbed out of a battered pickup, the standard mode of transportation for about ninety percent of the rural residents of Montana. He walked up the sidewalk toward the entrance of the building.

Collin Kincaid. Handsome, as all the Kincaid men were. Eyes like blue sapphires. Dark, almost-black, hair. Half a foot taller than her own five-seven stature, giving him the height advantage even when she wore high heels. He was also muscular. His palm had been calloused when they had shaken hands at their first meeting. He was a working rancher, not an armchair cowboy.

Collin was also the only legitimate grandson of Garrett Kincaid. Garrett was trying to buy the old Kincaid spread from the trustees who managed the ranch for seven-year-old Jenny McCallum, the heir to the throne, so to speak. The grandfather wanted to provide a legacy for the other six grandsons—a seventh hadn't been found yet but was thought to exist—all of whom were the bastard offspring of Garrett's deceased son, Larry Kincaid.

Oh, what tangled webs we weave…

Not just Larry with his profligate womanizing, she mused, but all humans. She gave a snort of amusement. My, but she was waxing philosophical today.

Because Collin Kincaid made her nervous? Because she'd felt the unmistakable pull of male-female interest between them the first time they'd met? Because they were enemies?

Impatient with her thoughts, she resumed her seat in the executive chair and pulled herself closer to the desk. It was an effective shield, she'd found, for dealing with those who didn't take her seriously as an attorney.

The secretary—another indication, along with the sign and new building, of the corporation's affluent image, one her father wanted to project these days—buzzed her on the intercom and announced Kincaid's arrival.

"Send him in," she requested. She didn't stand when the door opened. Keeping her seat kept her in the position of authority. In this office, she was the one in charge.

His eyes crinkled at the corners when he smiled upon seeing her. Their startling blue depths held laughter as he advanced across the Oriental carpet, as if he knew more than he was telling. And saw more than she was willing to reveal.

He was dressed in a gray summer suit with a touch of blue in the weave. His shirt was white and immaculate, his tie a tasteful blend of blue and gray with a touch of red.

Understated. Nothing too obvious, yet he had an aura of power that could have been intimidating had a person less confidence in his or her own abilities.

She returned his smile with cool professionalism.

He had a way of acting older and more experienced in the ways of the world than she, but that was ridiculous. He was only thirty-one to her almost twenty-eight. She'd gone to college at one of the prestigious Ivy League schools back east while he'd attended a Montana university. She'd been raised in New York until her father had decided to move back to Whitehorn a few years ago. Collin had lived most of his life on a ranch. Except for a few years with his mom and stepfather in San Diego after his parents divorced.

She wondered if that had been a lonely time for him. He'd returned to his grandfather's ranch over in Elk Springs when he was fourteen or thereabouts, so the town gossips had reported. He'd been a rebel at the time, but hard work and a firm hand from his grandfather had soon put him to rights, the local story went.

Not that Hope cared in the least about Collin's past, but knowledge of one's enemy was a good thing. She cleared her throat and nodded firmly.

"Good morning. Please be seated," she invited briskly, gesturing to the guest chair at the opposite side of the desk. Her tone was crisp, decisive.

He casually pulled the chair to the side of the desk, angling it toward her, then sat and stretched out his long legs so that his black dress boots were within two feet of her chair.

This action encroached on her space and forced her to angle her chair sideways to face him in a full frontal position, which she favored as one of greater power. It also put her feet within touching range of his, which further decreased the autonomy of her position.

"So," he said in his deep, pleasant baritone, "we meet again."

There was a world of innuendo in the statement. As if they'd been lovers or something in the not-too-distant past.

"Yes," she said coolly, and picked up the Kincaid file. She flipped it open and studied the first page without really seeing it. Realizing she was using the folder as a shield, she tossed it back onto the desk, disgusted with her cowardice. "I don't see that we have anything more to discuss," she said, deftly reminding him that he had been the one to request the meeting.

"Don't you?" he inquired with lazy humor.

He laid his creamy white Stetson hat, which he'd been holding, on her credenza. She was chagrined with herself for not telling him to hang it on the antique lowboy beside her door. Now he was further ensconced in her space.

In fact, she was beginning to feel surrounded by his confident masculinity. His eyes, as blue as the Montana sky, studied her. There was nothing lazy or humorous in that probing perusal. Her heart beat faster as she shifted uneasily in the executive chair.

Annoyed, she told him, "Past meetings between our parties have not been productive."

"Well," he drawled in that maddening Western accent, "your dad and my grandfather tend to get a mite heated on the subject. I thought you and I could discuss a possible settlement more fully without them being present."

His eyes raked over her navy-blue coat dress that fastened all the way down the front with red-and-white enameled buttons. He lingered at the last button, which was located four inches above the hemline. Her knee was visible in the slit thus created.

Hope pulled her chair close to the desk so that her legs were hidden and twisted sideways from the waist so she could face him. "Does this mean you're accepting our terms for settling the case?"

He had the nerve to laugh. The crinkles appeared beside his eyes again and twin lines indented his lean cheeks. His teeth were very white in contrast to his tanned face. His lips curved alluringly at the corners. She stared at his mouth and wondered about his kiss, how it would feel, if his lips would be hard or tender as he touched hers—

Appalled, she broke the thought and brought her wayward mind back to what he was saying.

"Hardly. My grandfather would have apoplexy. He's determined to provide a legacy for his other grandsons and has decided the Kincaid ranch here in Whitehorn is the perfect place. The way I see it, we can haggle over this for years in the courts and not do anyone any good, or we can iron out an agreement."

"What is your idea of an agreement?"

"That Jordan buy what's left of the old Baxter ranch from the trustees at the price they offered it to us and let the rest go."

Hope knew her father would never agree to anything less than the total original Baxter land. "Your grandfather has agreed to this?" she asked, probing for information.

"Well, not exactly. He's as stubborn as your father. The Baxter place was folded into the Kincaid spread years ago. Granddad wants to keep the ranch intact as it now stands."

"The sale of those two parcels was illegal since the original acquisition of the Baxter land was accomplished through fraudulent means," she reminded him.

He heaved a sigh. "Looks like we're going to talk in circles."

She stood. "Then there's no need to continue this meeting, is there?"

He rose, too, a frown marring his good looks. "My idea was that if we each took the same proposition to your dad and my grandfather, maybe we could get them to agree. A year of haggling over this is more than enough."

His nearness bothered her. Standing no more than

two feet away, she could feel the blanket of warmth from his body and the aura of confidence that came from the supreme ego that all the Kincaid men seemed to possess. She could smell soap and sandalwood talc and aftershave.

She became dizzy, the air suddenly close, hot and still. Stepping back, she bumped into her chair, causing her knees to buckle. "Oh!"

With the quickness of a cat, his arms were there to steady her. She was engulfed by his heat, his scent, the protective cage of his arms and body.

"Easy," he murmured, his breath soft against the hair at her temple, his voice deep and gentle.

Laying her hands against his chest, she made the mistake of looking up at him. Instead of pushing away as she'd intended, she was trapped within the depths of his eyes. Blue was supposed to be a cool color, but that wasn't true of him. His gaze was blue…and hot. It burned down to some point in her that was suddenly agitated.

She felt the quick lift of his chest in a sharply indrawn breath, then the way he went very still, not releasing her, yet not taking advantage of their forced closeness.

His lips, the bottom one slightly fuller than the top, parted. His head bent toward hers.

A quick, sharp need rose from that disturbed place inside her and made her tingle where they touched. She moistened her lips, then realizing what she was doing, clamped them tightly shut. Directing a glare his way, she tried to step back but was trapped between him and the chair.

Panic, strange and harsh and lightning-fast, swept over her. Her breath caught. "Let me go," she ordered.

A second, an eternity, went by.

She was aware of a struggle in him, one as elemental as the hunger in herself that shocked and angered her sense of rightness. He was the enemy. She had to remember that.

He stepped back, sliding his hands from her back to her elbows to make sure she had her balance. "There now," he murmured as if soothing a nervous filly.

Shoving the chair aside, she retreated a full three feet away. "I will present your offer to my father," she told him stiffly. She sounded breathless, which she didn't like. It might be interpreted as weakness on her part.

"We haven't really discussed an offer yet. We'd better consider every facet and nail the details down before we jump in." He picked up his hat. "It's nearly noon. Let's review it over lunch."

"I really don't have time—"

"It's been a long spell since breakfast. I can't talk on an empty stomach. The Hip Hop okay with you?"

She hesitated, not sure she wasn't being rushed into something she would regret. However, her father wanted progress on the case and the courts liked to see a show of cooperation, so maybe she'd better go along with this arrogant Kincaid who seemed to think he could persuade her to his view. Besides, it was noon and her breakfast of toast with peanut butter was long gone, too.

"Yes, that will be fine." She was pleased that she spoke in a firm tone. She sounded in charge once more, her panic of a moment ago subdued.

His ready smile lit his face. "Great."

His hat in one hand, he placed the other under her elbow to escort her out. She gracefully eased away and retrieved her purse from the bottom desk drawer. She settled the strap over her shoulder and slipped the file folder into a soft-sided briefcase. Thus armed, she nodded that she was ready.

He stepped back and allowed her to precede him out of the office. She told her secretary where they would be and reiterated it to Kurt Peters, another full-time attorney with Baxter Development, when they encountered him in the quiet, cool hallway of the executive floor. With Collin observing every detail of the place, she was suddenly pleased with the show of Baxter wealth. While it didn't match that of the Kincaids, it wasn't something to be ignored, either.

"Shall I join you?" Kurt asked, his light blue eyes expressionless as he glanced at Collin.

Hope knew Kurt had absorbed her father's dislike of the Kincaids, which bordered on the obsessive.

A flicker of guilt shot through her at the disloyal thought. At eighteen, her father had been cheated of his birthright as the promised heir to the Baxter ranch, which was owned by his uncle, Cameron Baxter, at that time.

Jeremiah Kincaid, former owner of the Kincaid ranch and a cousin to the present Kincaids who were trying to buy the place from Jenny's trustees, had pulled strings to get the bank notes on the Baxter land called, thus forcing Cameron to sell or go into bankruptcy. Jeremiah had then bought the place for a song.

"This is a private conversation," Collin said to Kurt before she could reply, taking her arm again and leading her past the other lawyer.

"I'll talk to you later," she called over her shoulder to Kurt. "Don't push me around," she said when she and Collin were out of hearing.

"I wouldn't think of it," he returned smoothly and, opening the door, ushered her out into the August heat.

At his truck, Collin considered helping Hope inside with the simple expedient of putting his hands on her waist and lifting her, but thought better of it.

Admiration hit him as she solved the problem of the high step by reaching down and unfastening the bottom button of her dress. Then she grabbed the handhold inside the door, stepped up with her left foot and swung neatly inside, her shapely behind plopping gracefully onto the leather seat.

His libido stampeded all over his self-control.

He closed the door and went around to the driver's side. The heat was suffocating. He cranked up the engine and flipped the air conditioner on high. They were silent on the short drive to the main street of town. He pulled over to the curb on a side street beside the town park. She climbed out before he could get around to help her.

At the Hip Hop Café, they were directed to a table for two by the window where they could look out on the busy street or beyond to the hilly terrain east of town. Ranchers called out greetings as they wound their way through the busy diner. He noted their quick speculative glances at Hope and their equally quick nods.

Outsiders were viewed with suspicion in these parts. Her father had been buying up land in the county for years, even before he moved back here, which caused resentment among the old-timers. Collin noted the lift of her chin and the way she smiled at one and all. He mentally grinned. This woman had spirit. She wouldn't be intimidated by a bunch of clannish ranchers.

A new waitress had replaced Emma Stover, nee Baxter, who was now his sister-in-law by virtue of marrying Brandon Harper, one of his newly discovered half-brothers. The lives of the Kincaid brothers were getting complicated.

The Baxters seemed to be at the heart of the complications, largely because of the controversy over the ranch and the lawsuit, which threatened to drag on forever. And of course, there was the matter of the new wives and babies being added to the Kincaid family at an awesome rate.

He felt a hitch in the vicinity of his heart. His granddad had made it plain that he expected Collin to marry and populate their ranch in Elk Springs, Montana, with a new generation of Kincaids. The sooner, the better. Seeing the domestic bliss of his half brothers brought the same thought to his mind. Now all he needed was a willing woman.

His gaze was drawn to his companion who was studying the menu with the grave seriousness she apparently brought to everything she did.

He frowned and peered at the menu he held. Getting mixed up with a woman whose father was a sworn enemy of the family would be stupid beyond belief. But, he had to admit, something about her fascinated him, this beautiful enemy who was as aware of him as he was of her.

"Are you ready to order?" the pretty young waitress inquired, her pad and pencil ready.

"Hmm, it's Tuesday," he recalled. "The blue plate special is elk hash, isn't it?"

"Yes, sir." She read the day's special, which was written on a chalkboard near the cash register, as if he couldn't read or maybe couldn't see that far.

He frowned. The young woman evidently thought he was ancient. Catching the brief curving of Hope's mouth before she sternly disciplined the mirth at his expense, he grinned and winked at her

before ordering the special and a glass of rasp-
berry iced tea.

"I'll have the same," she said, handing the menu
to the teenage waitress and settling back in the chair,
her eyes on the traffic moving slowly along the street.
"Superior court is in session," she noted.

"Mmm-hmm. I see Judge Kate Randall Walker in
a booth with the local psychic. Wonder where Lily
Mae Wheeler is. She's usually holding court here in
the Hip Hop at noon everyday."

This time Hope did smile. She even laughed, a tiny
gurgle of sound that enchanted him. She was a mystery,
this woman, one he would like very much to unravel.
He backed off from the thought. She had pretty much
made it clear that she, like her father, wouldn't give a
Kincaid the time of day if she could avoid it.

"I'm glad Emma was cleared of that murder charge,"
Hope murmured. "It's so odd to find a new relative, to
learn my father and Emma's mother are first cousins,
after all these years of thinking there was no one else."

"The notorious Lexine Baxter," Collin said, refer-
ring to Emma's mother, who evidently killed anyone
who stood in the way of her ambitions, including a
former partner, a husband, and finally Jeremiah
Kincaid, her father-in-law. The woman was now in
prison for her crimes.

A blush highlighted the porcelain skin of his dining
companion as if she was embarrassed at the mention
of her infamous relative. Collin couldn't look away.

Hope Baxter was a natural blonde. Her eyes were large and of a soft blue-gray with a hint of vulnerability buried deep in them that was at odds with her cool, professional manner. Sometimes he thought he detected a hint of sadness in her. It made him wonder about her life.

With divorced parents and a profligate father he could never depend on, Collin knew how a person's family could cause wounds that were hard to heal, if they ever did. His grandfather, Garrett Kincaid, had taken him in hand when he was fourteen and probably saved him from a senseless life of dissipation similar to his father's.

"Sorry," he murmured. "I didn't mean to pull your family skeletons out of the closet."

"I never knew Lexine. My father never mentioned her. So she doesn't really seem like family." She paused and looked troubled. "I would like to know Emma, though. I always wanted a sister. It's lonely, growing up with no relatives. My father was always so busy—"

She stopped abruptly, looking surprised and irritated with herself, as if she'd given away family secrets. She was very protective of her father. Collin had seen that in the brief meetings with the older men present, meetings that more than once had ended in anger and a shouting match between her father and his granddad.

Collin mentally shook his head. He didn't have much hope of doing any better than his grandfather, but he had promised he would try. If only he could find a way to breach the barriers he sensed in her....

"Your father doesn't have a chance of winning this case," he said, switching back to the subject of their meeting. "His claim is too old. He should have pursued it at the time of the sale to Jeremiah."

"He didn't have the means then." She directed a hard look his way. "Nor the evidence we have now. Jeremiah made sure of that."

"We both have interesting characters in our respective families," he said with grim humor. Jeremiah Kincaid had been a womanizer just as his own father had been. However, unlike Larry with his six, maybe seven, illegitimate kids, Jeremiah had only two that they knew of.

She ignored his attempt to put them on common ground. Her face stern, she reminded him, "There is no statute of limitations on fraud."

"Yeah, I remember that from business law."

He had studied business management from a ranching viewpoint. Business law had focused on land ownership and legal decisions involving ranches and cattle disputes, or the inheritance of those.

"Then you must admit we have a very strong case," Hope said. "It would be in your family's interests to settle it now."

He couldn't help the sardonic tinge in his voice. "Well, now, if it were up to me, I would, but with the sale of those two parcels—one of which was to the

Laughing Horse Reservation—others are involved.
Jackson Hawk says the res won't give up the land.
They're too far along with plans for a resort on it."

Her eyes turned frosty. "That land belongs to my
father. The trustees had no right to sell it. Surely
with the famous Kincaid influence and charm, your
grandfather can persuade the tribal elders to give up
their claim. I'm sure the Kincaids can afford to
return their money."

"With interest," he agreed, his own tone hardening.

The waitress arrived with their food, forestalling
the argument. Damn, but he was tired of this whole
thing. They had been at a stalemate for months. What
made his granddad think *he* could break through the
impasse? Baxter's daughter was as tough and stubborn as her old man.

Silence engulfed them when they were alone
again. He began eating the meal, one of his favorites,
without tasting it. When the door of the café opened,
he watched the new arrivals with a jaundiced eye. He
recognized the woman as a local florist and wedding
planner. She carried her son in her arms.

The kid, who looked about two years old, glanced
his way and shouted, "Ope. Ope."

Collin felt decidedly uncomfortable, as if the boy
had named him the absent and unknown father of the
florist's son. Heat suffused his ears.

The woman laughed and came toward him. Hell,
what was going on?

"Hope," she said to her son. "Hope."

"Ope. Ope," the boy said.

Hope laughed, startling him. It was a truly joyous sound, a welcoming sound rather than an amused gurgle. He was instantly fascinated. She held out her arms.

For a second Collin thought heaven had opened its gates and was inviting him inside. He was totally fascinated by the change in her. Whereas a moment ago she'd been all frosty professionalism, there was now tenderness and laughter in her eyes. But she wasn't looking at him. He swallowed hard and watched the woman with the kid stop at the table.

"Here, he's yours." The mother dumped the child into Hope's willing embrace. "Gabe can say 'Ope,' but can't seem to get the *H* on the front of Hope," she explained to Collin.

"Hey, big boy," Hope murmured.

"Shug," the child said in an insistent voice.

"You have some sugar for me?" she asked in make-believe surprise, her eyes going wide.

The kid nodded and grinned happily.

To Collin's further amazement, the cool, serious attorney planted loud, smacking kisses on the toddler's neck and ear until he giggled with delight. The kid caught chubby fists in her smooth hair and left it in tangles when she settled him on her lap.

Seeing his gaze on them, the blush hit her cheeks again. "This is Meg Reilly and her son, Gabe. Have you two met?" Hope asked, reverting to the polite persona he suddenly disliked.

"No, we haven't. Glad to meet you," he said.

"You're Collin, right?" Meg asked. "It's hard to keep all the Kincaid brothers straight. Oh, I'm sorry. That was extremely rude of me."

With green eyes and wavy brown hair, she was a pretty woman a few years older than he. He liked her rueful smile and straightforward manner when she apologized.

"No problem," he assured her. "I had trouble keeping the names straight myself when it was discovered I had six half brothers."

Her frank gaze was discerning. "That must have been a startling revelation."

"To put it mildly."

"From all evidence, you've handled it well." She turned to her son who was playing some kind of clapping game with Hope. "Okay, young man, I know you hate to leave the love of your young life, but Mommy needs to eat. It's been a hectic morning with a bridal shower and two funerals," she explained to the adults.

"Who's dead?" Collin asked.

Sorrow rippled over her face. "A baby that was stillborn, and the son of a rancher who lives at the far northern reaches of the county. The son was from New York. He was in advertising and dropped dead of a heart attack in a meeting with a client. His father brought him back here to be buried in the family cemetery."

"It must be terrible to lose a child," Hope said, handing the boy to Meg. Her eyes were as soft as velvet.

"Yes," Meg agreed after a beat of silence. "See you later. Don't forget you're coming to supper Thursday night."

"I won't."

Watching Hope with her friend, Collin had an idea. He considered it from every angle, looking for flaws and planning an argument to win her to the plan, which, in his estimation, was a sound one.

When Meg and Gabe left them to sit at the counter, he ate the tasty hash and studied Hope for a moment before speaking what was on his mind.

"I think you should come out to the ranch and look the land over before presenting our offer to your father. That way you'll know exactly what we're talking about. I can show you the two parcels in dispute."

He liked the way her eyes opened wide as surprise darted through them. He waited impatiently for her answer.

Two

"No," Hope said, sounding as horrified as she felt.

She had done some stupid things in her life, such as getting mixed up with a fortune hunter in law school, but becoming involved with Collin Kincaid wasn't going to be added to the list. She knew all about his father and the women the man had seduced—there were six known bastard sons to verify that. She wasn't going to allow herself to be seduced by the current Kincaid heir. Going to the ranch with Collin would be the first step on that slippery slope.

"It would be logical," he insisted, leaning forward over the table, his expression serious.

"'Logical'?" she questioned. That was the last word she would have expected him to use.

"Sure. You can view the two parcels that were sold, then you'll know exactly what you're talking about when you approach your father with our offer. Or don't you care to see the land you're fighting so hard over?"

The sardonic undertone hit a nerve. She had, of course, been out to the old Baxter spread. From what she could see, it was mostly hills and sharp peaks, but in truth she had only gone a short distance. The original ranch road had been too overgrown with shrubs and pine seedlings to navigate and the old mining road had been too rough for her car. A four-wheel-drive vehicle was the only practical way to get around in this country if one intended to really explore it in detail.

"And when I've seen it?" she inquired.

"Then, as a fully informed attorney, you can truly advise your father as to its value and if it's worth another year of wrangling over."

His tone as much as his words challenged her legal expertise. She stiffened in resentment.

But her next thought was that she wanted to see the ranch, not so much because of the case but because it was part of her history. The Baxter roots in Montana went back as far as the Kincaid roots did. Somehow her family had lost its heritage.

Somehow? She knew the "how" of that loss. Jeremiah Kincaid and his lying, cheating ways.

"What time shall I pick you up on Friday?" Collin asked, smoothly diverting her thoughts from the past.

"Pick me up?" she asked, puzzled. Had she lost track of the conversation?

"The old Baxter spread is a substantial piece of land. We'll need a couple of days to see it all. The weekend would be a good time for me. You can stay over at the ranch house. We have plenty of room."

He leaned back in the chair, as if sure that she would fall in with his plan, which would put her right in the middle of the Kincaid compound and the multiple relatives who now lived there as if it were already theirs.

"What arrogance," she said, keeping her voice soft, amused. "My father doesn't jump to your bidding. Neither do I. This lawsuit isn't going to be disposed of at the whim of the current Kincaid family. We're willing to pay top dollar for the Baxter place, which rightfully belongs to my family. Will the court believe the trustees are acting in Jennifer McCallum's best interest to sell for less?"

"If Jordan can pull that much money together. It seems to me he's spread pretty thin, what with all the developing he's doing south of town, plus, the fancy new headquarters building."

Collin's manner was coolly sardonic now, but edged with the Kincaid fury that was as well known as their legendary charm. She was angry, too. She didn't appreciate his trying to manipulate her into doing as he wanted, nor his casting doubts on her father's business acumen.

"My father has more than enough resources to handle the ranch sale, which has nothing to do with Baxter Development Corporation."

Unable to finish the meal, she laid her fork down and stood. Collin, polite as usual, immediately got to his feet, tall and intimidating.

"You Kincaids stick together like flies on honey, but you won't win this case," she informed him heatedly.

"Don't take that to the bank quite yet," he advised with an amused glance at the gaping faces around them.

A couple of ranchers chuckled openly while several of the local residents grinned behind their hands. Hope was the outsider, and she was acutely aware of that fact.

"I wouldn't think of it. I'll see you in court," she said, flashing him a breezy smile and answering the challenge in his eyes with a confident lift of her chin.

She walked out of the quaint café, aware of multiple stares as she did, and especially that of Collin Kincaid's.

Collin remained at the table, his face impassive as he observed her departure.

Outside, she spotted another employee of the corporation and got a ride to her office. There, she closed her door and paced restlessly to and fro, aware of a trembling deep inside her. She felt she'd braved the lion in his den and had gotten out alive—but not unscathed.

Sighing, she calmed herself and admitted she'd blown the meeting, walking out in a huff that way.

As if emotion ever solved anything. She was more angry with herself than with Collin. It was his job to persuade her to see things his way just as it was hers to see that things were settled in her father's favor.

Oh, what tangled webs…

Sitting at the desk, she pressed her forehand against her hands and wished this whole thing was over. She was so tired of the Baxter ranch and her father's obsession—

Biting back the rest of the disloyal thought, she rubbed her temples where a headache pinged insistently. She removed the folder from her briefcase and again studied the facts in minute detail. Yes, they definitely had a case.

She wondered if she could get the venue changed to Great Falls or Billings. She would have to show a higher court that the local judge could be prejudiced in favor of the Kincaids. If she lost, though, the case would go that much harder for her side.

Before she could think this through, the door opened. Only her father would dare intrude without an announcement. She looked up and met his eyes.

"Good afternoon, Father."

"What's this I hear about you having lunch with the Kincaid grandson?"

Her father refused to recognize any of the bastard grandsons, so for him there was only one—Collin, the legal heir to Garrett Kincaid's holdings.

"I thought I told you I had a meeting with Collin

today." She knew she had. She was also pretty sure she knew who had mentioned the luncheon to her dad. Kurt Peters curried her father's favor in every way he could.

"What did he say?"

She considered how much to tell him, not just the facts, but the nuances of the meeting. "They're tired of wrangling over the land. They'll ask the trustees to sell us the remainder of the Baxter land for the price they offered it to Garrett Kincaid."

Her father's face darkened dangerously. "They'll sell *all* the Baxter land to me."

"Jackson Hawk is representing the reservation. Collin said their plans are too far along to stop. I've spoken with Hawk prior to this. The tribal elders refuse to give up the land and will press their own suit if need be."

"Have they started building?" he demanded.

"I don't know. Legally, it doesn't matter to our case. By buying land without a clear title, they aren't entitled to any special consideration. However, their suit will complicate things for us."

Her father sat on the corner of her desk, another perk only he was allowed. "Those blasted Indians. We need to check on what they're doing. I have to fly to New York tomorrow on that bank merger since I'm on the board of directors. You'll have to go out there."

Surprised at this announcement, she said, "Collin invited me to spend the weekend at the Kincaid place. He thought I should look the Baxter land over. That sounds like a case of 'Come into my parlor, said the spider to the fly,' doesn't it?" She smiled in ironic amusement.

Instead of seeing the humor in the idea of her being at the Kincaid compound, surrounded by their opponents and those loyal to them, her father slapped his hand on his thigh and chortled.

"Good," he said. "Perfect. When do you go?"

Her jaw nearly sagged at his elation. "I turned him down. Why would I fall in with his plans?"

"Why? To see what's going on. You can check on the reservation doings at the same time since the land adjoins the Kincaid place." He gave her a derisive glare. "Where's your head, girl? You might be able to come up with something we've overlooked or know nothing about. We need to know any weakness in their case or if they have any surprises up their sleeves."

"We've already gone into disclosure," she reminded him.

"I'm not talking about legal stuff," he interrupted, silencing her in his usual impatient manner. "We need to look for chinks in the family armor. Or among the ranch hands. Not everyone out there thinks the Kincaids are God's gift to Montana. Someone working on the ranch might have information we can use."

She remained silent, every instinct within her advising that this was the wrong thing to do.

"Call the grandson and tell him you accept."

She stood. Her manner cool and at odds with the way she felt inside, she said, "I'll consider it."

His eyebrows shot up. She'd never used that particular tone with him. She didn't know why she felt so defensive.

For once he seemed at a loss for words. "Well, then, good." He glanced at his watch. "I've got to go to a meeting on the new mall in five minutes. Blasted construction boss is a crook, if you ask me. I'll see you Monday when I get back from New York. No, Tuesday here at the office."

"All right."

She remained standing behind her desk after he'd gone. She doubted he heard her agreement. It would never occur to him that she wouldn't be there or that she might have other things to do. For the briefest second, resentment stormed through her, causing a lump to form in her throat.

The telephone rang, diverting her from the strange tempest of emotion. She cleared her throat and answered. For the rest of the afternoon, she was too busy to think. At six, she went to her apartment in one of the elite Baxter Development complexes. A common-interest development or C.I.D., as it was called in the industry, it was inhabited by professional couples or those wealthy enough to afford a second home.

The mountains around Whitehorn were scenic and

the fact that the town was close to Yellowstone was an added attraction for those with children. The county was becoming increasingly popular with families from metropolitan areas.

Her father had seen the opportunities long ago. The fact that the local people hadn't certainly wasn't his fault. Pulling on her bathing suit, she wondered why she sometimes felt a twinge of guilt as the company bought up mismanaged ranches and turned them into thriving strip malls, condos, golf courses and nature trails for the aging baby boomers. The mismanagement wasn't her father's fault.

Swimming one hundred laps of the Olympic-size indoor pool, she dreaded the thought of calling Collin and accepting his offer. It felt like a concession on her part, which could be interpreted as a sign of weakness from their side. Neither did she like the idea of being a spy sent into the enemy camp by her father.

She sighed shakily. She felt she no longer knew the man she'd adored as a child. They were becoming more and more estranged. It bothered her.

From what she had seen of Collin and his grandfather, they were very close-knit. For a second, something like envy washed through her. She discarded the notion and put her efforts into propelling herself through the water that was almost as warm as a bathtub.

At the end of an hour, feeling neither refreshed nor any happier, she returned to her place. The silence seemed to mock her as she showered and dressed in silk pajamas, then ate a salad for dinner.

She wondered how many of the grandsons and their various families were at the Kincaid spread and imagined them crowded around a long table, laughing while Collin told them about the meeting.

Collin returned to the dining room and the lunch he'd left to answer a summons to the phone. "Will wonders never cease?" he said to his grandfather, the seventy-three-year-old patriarch of the Elk Springs branch of the Kincaids. "Yesterday Hope Baxter refused to accept an invitation to come out and look the ranch over. Today she calls and says she will."

Garrett beamed. "I knew the Kincaid charm wouldn't fail," he said cheerfully.

Collin had his doubts about that. It wasn't charm that had changed Hope's mind about coming out for the weekend. Whatever it was, he figured he could find out before the weekend was over. He would make a point of it.

"What's happening?" Trent, one of Larry Kincaid's other illegitimate sons, wanted to know.

"Collin talked Baxter's daughter into coming out to the ranch. She'll be here for the weekend," Garrett told him.

Trent glanced first at his wife Gina and then back at Collin with interest. "She's the attorney on the case, isn't she?"

Collin nodded and didn't add anything more.

"It's strange how the Kincaid family seems to be so totally enmeshed with the Baxters, isn't it?" Trent continued. "Lexine, Emma's birth mother, was married to Dugin Kincaid, Jeremiah's younger son. Now Emma is married to Brandon, a Kincaid from the illegitimate branch of the family."

"And has a twin, although Emma's mother isn't admitting to having another child," Gina, the private investigator instrumental in locating Garrett's grandsons, reminded them.

The DNA tests that had nearly convicted Emma in the death of the mayor's daughter, Christina Montgomery, had proven she was one of a set of identical twins. Only the fact that Emma'd been inoculated against rubella and her mysterious twin hadn't, had saved her.

Collin thought of Hope and her embarrassment at the mention of her relative, the notorious Lexine Baxter.

The unknown twin, who had apparently been with Christine Montgomery shortly before her death, wasn't making herself accessible to the local authorities as requested through the news media. From what he'd seen of Brandon's wife, Emma wasn't anything like her mother. Was the twin?

Gina laughed ruefully. "So. Does this mean there's going to be one more for dinner this weekend?"

"I'll help with the cooking," Trent volunteered.

Hattie, their previous housekeeper, had recently quit. The ranch had trouble keeping help because of

the supposed curse on the Kincaid land. Gina had
assumed most of the planning and served as executor
of household chores. Everyone had been assigned a
task that contributed to the running of the homestead.

There were moans all around and graphic remin-
ders of charred hamburgers resembling charcoal bri-
quettes at Trent's last attempt at supper. He was
unrepentant. "Practice makes perfect."

"Only if you do it right," Collin told him. "You
have to keep an eye on the grill and squirt water on
the flames *before* they incinerate the burgers."

"Hey, I can do it," Trent assured everyone.

"Uh-oh," Gina said, "the impatient one awakes."
She hurried from the table to answer her son's
summons.

Collin's grandfather chuckled. "I believe women
could hear the cry of their own baby if they were at
a ball game with fifty-thousand cheering fans and the
child was in a nursery a mile away." He turned his
gaze on Collin. "It's about time you were thinking of
starting your family. You aren't getting any younger."

"I'm only thirty-one," Collin protested good-naturedly. He'd been hearing about marriage and children
from the old man since he could remember. "Besides,
I'm too busy rushing back and forth between here
and Elk Springs to think about finding a bride."

Across the table, his half brother watched with the
assured grin of one who had done his part and won
their grandfather's approbation by acquiring a wife

and providing a son to carry on the Kincaid tradition in Whitehorn.

Assuming they ever got title to the ranch.

Collin frowned as he recalled his brief telephone conversation with Hope. He wanted to know what had happened to change her mind between their meeting yesterday, which hadn't gone well in his opinion, and this morning.

She had been positively horrified at the idea when he had mentioned it yesterday at lunch at the Hip Hop Café. Today she'd admitted he was probably right— she needed to see the land to know exactly what parcels had been sold off the original Baxter holdings. She was a mystery, this woman who'd had the nerve to walk out on him in the busy diner one day, then call him the next, pretty as you please, to admit she'd possibly been wrong.

A thrum of anticipation vibrated through him. It had nothing to do with settling the case and everything to do with being alone with her as they explored the range.

Alarms went off in his head, but he knew he wasn't going to heed them. Ruefully he wondered what had happened to his instinct for survival.

"So what's the plan?" Trent wanted to know.

Collin shook his head. "No particular plan. I thought she should come out and explore the place while we try to hammer down the details of an offer that her father, we hope, can't refuse."

Trent's face darkened. "Revenge. The man is

obsessed with it. That's the only reason for this whole lawsuit."

"It's hard to let go of a dream," Garrett said sadly. "He was promised the place as a teenager. He poured his heart into it, then it was lost to him through no fault of his own. That's a deep hurt."

Collin studied his grandfather. The old man had a temper, which had exploded in the last meeting with Jordan Baxter and his sharp-minded daughter, but he also understood the underlying emotion of his enemy. Collin hoped when he was his grandfather's age he had half the understanding of human nature that Garrett had. And the compassion.

Collin had at first been resentful of the brood of bastard brothers, but that was before he'd realized he'd had life a lot easier than any of them. He'd known his roots. And he'd had Garrett's unwavering love to help him on the right path. That had been the greatest influence in his life.

Realizing his advantages and that the Elk Springs ranch would still be his—and his sister's, of course—he'd pitched in to help the new brothers gain their own part of the Kincaid inheritance. He'd even learned to like them for the most part, especially Trent, who was becoming a close friend.

Both Trent and Gina liked staying at the ranch and did so often. Cade and Leanne had built a fine house in a wooded meadow nearby. Brandon and Emma were thinking of doing the same. Emma and

Hope, newly discovered cousins, could get to know each other…

Shocked at the direction of his thoughts, Collin broke off the odd musing. Rising, he told his grandfather, "I have work to do. I need to talk to Cade on the Appaloosa breeding program. I saw a stallion on the res the other day that he might be interested in."

Garrett nodded, his smile serene.

Although the lawsuit wasn't over, Collin knew his grandfather thought things were progressing smoothly and according to plan—which was to have all his grandsons married and settled within the year.

That left him as the last Kincaid bachelor. Plus the unknown seventh bastard son of Larry Kincaid.

Gina had traced his philandering father's whereabouts at the time and was sure the last son had been conceived and still existed in Whitehorn. It was only a matter of time before she found the woman who'd been involved, Gina'd said. She was checking birth records in Whitehorn, plus Blue River County and all connecting counties.

The seventh son would still be a child, though. Garrett would have to wait a number of years before he could be married off.

Smiling, Collin headed across the compound to the horse arena where Cade was sure to be working with his prize Appaloosas. He wondered if his weekend guest liked to ride. That was how he intended to show her around the place.

At the thought of being alone with Hope for hours out on the trail, his body stirred hungrily. She was a beautiful woman. A man would have to be deaf, dumb and blind to not respond to her.

She was also an enigma. There was something soft and alluring, totally feminine, about her that came across in spite of her cool professionalism.

The picture of Hope holding the toddler in her lap came to him. In spite of her lawyerly ways, she couldn't hide the other facets to her personality. With the child, she'd been warm and exuberant and open, not minding at all if her hair was mussed or her dress wrinkled. There was no doubt in his mind that she would make an excellent mother.

Together they would produce beautiful children—

Again he was dumbfounded at the direction his mind had taken. He scoffed at his own wild imagination. There was no way in hell Hope Baxter would ever have anything to do with a Kincaid other than in court, fighting over some rocks and valleys that weren't much good for anything anyway.

He wasn't going to fall for her, either. No way.

But the attraction was there.

Yeah, sex. So what? An attraction didn't mean lasting commitment or anything serious. He'd made his share of mistakes in his life, but he certainly wasn't going to do anything as stupid as fall in love with her.

Three

Hope zipped Gabe into his one-piece pajama outfit, then lifted him into her arms and sat in the handy rocker. "Ready for a story?"

"Store," he said in his usual way of shortening all words to their most basic of syllables.

She opened the book and read the bedtime tale. The toddler was almost asleep when she finished. She rocked him for a few minutes more, reluctant to give up this sweet bundle of humanity just yet.

Closing her eyes, she waited for the pain that squeezed her chest to subside. She finally admitted what her heart had known for ages—she wanted a family of her own. She wanted a child as darling and special as Gabe had become to her. Unlike Meg, who declared she was happy on her own, Hope envisioned another person—someone wonderful—who would share that home with her. That someone had never crossed her path, not in almost twenty-eight years. She thought he never would.

Sighing, she rose carefully, put the sleeping baby into the crib and lifted the side into place. She returned to the living room where Meg sat on the sofa sipping a cup of tea. "Want one?" she asked.

"I'll get it." Hope poured a cup of herb tea and settled in a chair, another rocker. She glanced around the pleasant room whose every corner was crowded with plants. White lace curtains framed a window lined with violets. She sighed, kicked her shoes off and curled into the chair.

This was the one place she felt totally at ease. Meg was her best friend in Whitehorn. Her only friend, really, besides an old high school and college pal back in New York where she'd grown up.

Her fault, she supposed. She didn't readily open up to people. Maybe that was a result of growing up without a mother and trying to please a father who had wanted a son to carry on the family enterprises. She sighed again. Her heart felt so strangely heavy of late.

"That's the umpteenth heavy sigh I've heard from you tonight," Meg commented. "What's on your little mind?"

"Not much," Hope admitted.

"The lawsuit? I assume that was the topic of conversation between you and Collin Kincaid when I saw you two at the Hip Hop on Tuesday."

"Yes." Hope gazed pensively at her friend. Meg was thirty-five, older and, if not wiser, then at least with a better perspective on life than *she* had. Hope could use some perspective right now. "Collin invited me to the ranch for the weekend. I refused."

"And?"

"My father wants me to go. He wants me to, well, see if I can gather anything of use for the trial."

"To be his spy in their midst," Meg concluded.

"Yes. It bothers me—" She broke off, then gave a little laugh. "It isn't as if Collin doesn't know I'm the enemy. He thinks we can persuade his grandfather and my father to come to a settlement if we join forces."

"That sounds like a good idea. What point does it serve for things to drag on as they have this past year?"

Put that way, Hope thought it sounded logical for her to go to the ranch. "Perhaps it is worth a try."

Meg nodded, then surprised Hope with a wicked grin. "The Kincaids are good-looking men. If Collin invited me for a romantic weekend at one of the most famous ranches in Montana, I'd go in a minute. You never can tell what might happen." She waggled her eyebrows suggestively.

"Meg!"

"Don't look so shocked. I may be over thirty, but I still remember what a handsome man is good for."

Hope tried to look amused while the telltale blood

rushed to her face, betraying the restless dreams she'd had Tuesday and Wednesday nights. She dreaded going to bed when she returned to her condo.

"Ah," Meg said, delight showing in her smile. "So that's the problem. You're interested in the grandson."

"No, I'm not," Hope denied, "not at all. That is, not as a man…"

Then what? some traitorous part of her demanded.

She couldn't meet her friend's probing gaze as Meg studied her more closely.

"So, are you going to the ranch?"

Hope nodded. "I called Collin yesterday and told him I would. To look over the original Baxter holdings and the two parcels that were sold off," she added quickly.

"Go with a clear conscience," Meg advised, her tone gentle. "You're not deceiving anyone about your purpose."

Tears burned unexpectedly behind Hope's eyes. "Then you think it's okay? To go, I mean?"

Meg considered a minute, then nodded.

Hope couldn't understand the relief that spread through her like warm honey. "Since I've committed to it, I suppose I have to. Do you think I should buy some cowgirl boots and a fringed skirt?"

Laughing, she rose, gave Meg a warm smile and left the cozy cottage. The night wind swept down from the peaks to the west of them. The Crazies, as the locals called the rough, imposing range. Sometimes she thought her father had been crazy to return to this state. It seemed to cause him only grief and sad memories.

The wind's chill fingers roamed down her neck, inciting goose bumps. She hurried to her car and drove to the modern condo that had never felt like a home. But then, neither had the mansion her father had built on a bluff overlooking the town.

Collin was on hand to welcome Hope when she arrived at the sprawling Kincaid ranch on Saturday morning. Since they wouldn't have had much time for exploring after work on Friday, she had decided to drive out on Saturday. Collin had made it plain he was disappointed. She tried not to let that fact influence her when she parked at an old horse rail in front of the ranch-style house and got out of the car.

"Good morning. You're right on time," he said. "Come on, we're going to the arena."

Without further ado, he led the way across the dirt-and-gravel parking area in the center of the elegant Kincaid spread, past several barns, stables and outbuildings, toward a huge metal building that she soon realized was the arena.

Inside, a man and a woman were mounted on two horses with striking dark brown and white markings. The couple, who were close to her and Collin in age, were putting their mounts through several exercises.

"A training session," Collin murmured.

His breath fanned the tendrils at her temples as he leaned close. A shiver danced over her left arm.

"Their horses, are they Indian paints?"

"Appaloosa. See the distinctive rump markings? That's what sets them off from paints. The Appaloosa was developed by the Nez Pierce independently of other Plains horses."

"They're beautiful," she said sincerely, fascinated as the man and woman expertly moved the horses around the huge showring, backing, pivoting, bowing with one hoof daintily in front of the other.

"That's Cade Redstone, one of my half brothers, and his wife Leanne. Leanne's brother, Rand Harding, is the foreman here. Wayne Kincaid manages the place."

She nodded. She knew the names of all the Kincaids associated with the ranch, both the Jeremiah branch and the Garrett branch. Jeremiah's legal son, Wayne, and his illegitimate son, Clint Calloway, had refused a share in the inheritance that had then fallen to their half sister, Jenny McCallum. Along with Jenny's adoptive father, Sterling McCallum, the half brothers acted as trustees for the seven-year-old.

Then there were the six illegitimate sons of Larry Kincaid, Collin's father, who stood to inherit the land if Garrett's plans went through.

So much family. Envy rose in her, but she ignored it. She had everything she needed—a career that truly interested her, a two-bedroom condo, friends…

"These are being trained as parade horses," Collin told her, "for the Ringling Bros. and Barnum & Bailey circus."

"My father took me to one of their shows at Madison Square Garden one year. I was six. It was the most exciting day of my life." She stopped as her throat closed and memory crowded in.

"What?" Collin questioned, as if sensing the sudden emotion in her.

"Father took the whole day off from work. He got front-row seats for us and three of my schoolfriends. It was my birthday," she explained.

A clown had given her a bouquet of paper flowers while the emcee had announced her birthday. The crowd had clapped and cheered for her. She had been so excited.

It seemed so long ago, almost as if it had happened to another person. That child had been so full of expectations that day. She'd thought life couldn't possibly be more perfect. Her father. Her three best friends. The nice clown. How little it had taken to make that child glow.

"Let's get you settled, then you can change. I have a nice calm gelding picked out for you to—"

"Gelding? As for riding?" she interrupted.

"Yes." He gave her a studied glance. "How else did you think we were going to explore the ranch?"

"By truck. I didn't bring any riding clothes."

He surveyed her khaki slacks and white blouse. He

frowned when he came to her sandals. "You need boots, is all. Leanne or Gina can fix you up. Come on."

Taking her elbow, he returned to her car, retrieved her overnight case and escorted her into the cool interior of the ranch house. He placed her bag in a room, indicated that his room was right across the hall in case she needed him, then led the way to the kitchen.

"Gina," he said to a woman stirring a pot, "do you think you can fit Hope with some boots? Sneakers would be okay if we can't find boots that fit."

She laid the spoon aside and smiled at Hope. "I'm Gina Remmington, Trent's wife. You must be Hope Baxter. Welcome to chaotic acres where life changes before your very eyes."

"Very funny," Collin quipped, albeit with a broad grin for his sister-in-law. "Can you help us out?"

"Sure. Come with me," she invited Hope, and led the way to another bedroom. "Is this your first visit to the ranch?"

"Yes. I really don't want to put you out—"

"It's no bother." She eyed Hope. "We're close to the same size, or the size I was before my son was born," she added ruefully, opening a drawer in a bureau. "Here's some jeans. And a chambray shirt. It would be a shame to ruin that blouse. It looks expensive."

Hope glanced at the white silk shirt with its elaborate cut-work pattern along the front. It was another birthday gift from her father. Picked out by his secretary.

Dismissing the cynical thought, she tried on jeans and boots, which were too snug, then a pair of old, comfortable sneakers. She put on the work shirt.

Gina stuck a white straw cowboy hat on Hope's head. "Perfect," she said.

Hope stared at her reflection in the full-length mirror. She looked so different she hardly recognized herself. She laughed. "I look like a ranch gal."

Gina grinned and nodded. "Let's see if Collin will approve the transformation." She led the way along the hall. They heard voices in the living room and detoured there. "Tah-dah," she said, turning to present Hope.

Heat suffused Hope's cheeks as Collin, Garrett and another of the Kincaid brothers turned three pairs of identical blue eyes on her. She paused at the doorway.

"Miss Baxter," Garrett said warmly. "We're delighted that you could join us for the weekend."

"Please, call me Hope." She shook hands with him.

"This is another of my grandsons. Have you met Brandon?" The older man introduced them. "You and Brandon's wife, Emma, must be cousins."

"Yes. I've seen her…when she was at the Hip Hop, and then later at the…"

She didn't want to bring up the arrest and preliminary hearing in which Emma had been accused of murdering some poor young woman who'd turned out to be the mayor's daughter.

There was a tangled web if ever there was one, Hope mused sympathetically, reflecting on all she'd heard about Lexine and Emma. Emma's own mother, Lexine Baxter, had intimated Emma might be guilty. It must be worse to have a mother like that than to have none at all.

"At the hearing," Brandon finished the sentence for her. He smiled grimly and held out a hand. "Glad to meet you."

Guilt speared through Hope. Would he be glad if he knew she was there to hopefully get information to oust him and his kin from the Baxter part of the Kincaid ranch?

"Hope and Collin are working out an agreement on the lawsuit," Garrett said, bringing the facts into the open and easing her discomfort.

Brandon's eyes were cool and assessing. He wasn't as outgoing as Collin. He was a man who played his cards close to his chest, as the Western saying went. "Good," was all he said, but she could detect wariness in him.

She lifted her chin. She wasn't there under false pretenses. She did want to settle the suit in a fair and equitable manner. If she learned anything her father could use, that was fair, too. He was the injured party.

Collin stepped close. "Ready to go?" He turned to his grandfather. "I thought we'd ride up the ridge to the old mining road and over to the land Wayne and Carey own."

"Good idea," Garrett approved. "It's a far piece. Will you be back for dinner?"

"No. I thought we'd take a picnic, then head back here in time for supper."

Hope had learned that on a ranch "dinner" was lunch and "supper" was dinner when she'd moved here fresh out of law school six years ago to join her father's firm. The town residents used lunch and dinner for the noon and evening meals, though. It had taken her a while to figure out she had to interpret words in the context of the person speaking.

When Collin finished talking to his grandfather about a couple of problems at the Elk Springs ranch, he and she headed outside. Two horses were already saddled in a corral next to a weathered stable.

"You have ridden before, haven't you?" he asked.

"Yes. I had riding lessons as a child."

"Figured you had. One of those fancy riding academies with the English saddles and the hopping up and down when the horse trots?"

"Posting. Yes."

"Yeah, posting."

His expression was innocent, but she detected a gleam in his eye. She realized he was teasing her, as if he knew her riding had been confined to gentle trails along marked paths. Her heart beat fast as she swung up onto the gelding before he could offer to help. Looking over the rolling pastures in the valley and beyond to the sharp hills that skirted the mountains, she wondered where this trail would lead.

* * *

"This is beautiful."

Collin agreed. But he was watching his guest as she gazed at the vast valley with its lush, irrigated fields dotted with prime beef cattle and the golden acres where hay had been grown for winter forage.

She faced him. "Is your Elk Springs ranch like this?"

"Pretty much. It lies in a long narrow valley where three rivers come together and eventually flow into the Columbia River."

"And then into the Pacific," she murmured, gazing at the mountains to the west as if she could see beyond those lofty peaks to where the mighty Columbia descended into the ocean.

He had a fleeting impression of some deep longing hidden within her that was fighting to reach the surface. He sensed contradictions in this slender woman with her New York accent and breeding, her keen analytical mind, her unexpected tenderness.

The latter was a facet he'd seen only briefly when she'd held her friend's child. He wondered what it would be like to be the recipient of a thousand sweet kisses from her.

He shifted uncomfortably in the saddle as his jeans became too snug. His body reacted to the sight, sound, even the thought of her, but he would do better to remember that she was the enemy. She would use anything she could find to win the lawsuit for her father.

Damn, but he was tired of the whole messy situation.

"Be warned," he told her, being perfectly open, "I'll protect my grandfather in any way I can."

She blinked and turned from the view. Her expression didn't change as she studied him. "I know that," she finally said. "I'll do the same for my father."

He liked the raw honesty of her words. He liked the loyalty. He liked too damned much about her.

"Come on," he said, urging his mount forward. "We're now on the original Baxter land. This ridge is the dividing line. We'll ride up to the cabin Wayne and Carey own. It used to be a line shack for ranch hands to use overnight while out riding fences or during roundup. Wayne has added a couple of bedrooms and a modern bathroom. They stay out here most of the summer, then move back to town before winter sets in."

"She's a pediatrician, isn't she?"

"Yes, one of the best in the state. She did a bone marrow transplant from Wayne to Jenny McCallum when Jenny developed leukemia. It saved the girl's life."

"I see."

Collin stopped the gelding he rode and studied her. She had that vulnerable look again. "What's bothering you?"

She looked startled. "Nothing," she denied, then added on a softer note, "Jenny was lucky to have a brother, one who cared."

Collin sensed her loneliness and wondered about her life as the motherless child of a rich, busy man in a big, impersonal city. It was something to think about. He remained silent for the rest of the short trip to the cabin.

Carey and Wayne were there, working to clear pine and fir trees that had started to invade the clearing around the place.

"Hi," their daughter Sophie called. She held her baby brother's hand.

Collin introduced Hope to Carey, Wayne, Sophie and Wayne Junior. He saw her blue-gray eyes linger on the boy, a toddler somewhat older than her friend's child.

"Hop down and visit for a while," Carey invited. "We need a break. We have fresh cinnamon rolls."

"I helped make them," Sophie informed them. "Come on, bubba. Let's eat."

"Eat," the wiry youngster repeated, his blue eyes lighting up. He made a beeline for the cabin.

"His favorite word," Wayne said with a chuckle, coming forward to take the reins and lead the horses to a shady spot where they fell to munching grass around the base of a big Western red cedar.

Carey brought a platter of rolls to the porch, along with napkins and mugs of coffee. "Come sit a spell," she called to them.

They arranged themselves on the porch, legs dangling over the edge, while they ate the delicious treat.

Hope complimented Sophie and her mother on their cooking skills. "I'm just learning," she confessed. "I was at boarding school most of the time while growing up and never got a chance to cook. I've mastered spaghetti sauce so far and I can grill hamburgers."

"Mom lets me cook all the time," Sophie confided.

"Maybe you'll be a famous chef like Julia Child."

Sophie considered this, then shook her head. "I'm going to be an astronaut and fly all over like Princess Leia and save people from the bad guys who went over to the Dark Side the way Darth Vader did."

Hope was suitably impressed and agreed that sounded like an ideal career for a modern woman. Collin was impressed as Hope expertly discussed the *Star Wars* characters with the youngster.

Another facet of her conflicting images, one who loved romantic space fiction, he mused. What other layers were hidden beneath her professional exterior?

The hot stirring in his blood urged him to try to find out. The attraction between them was strong, and not only on his side. Each time their eyes met, awareness leaped between them. He grimly beat the hunger into submission.

"What's happening at the hospital?" he asked Carey when Sophie dashed inside to get her latest *Star Wars* action figure to show Hope.

"Nothing good. Gavin has been put on leave pending the trial for Christina's murder." Carey looked grim. "Gavin is dedicated to healing. I can't believe he would hurt anyone."

Gavin Nighthawk, Collin knew, had recently been arrested for the murder of Christina Montgomery, daughter of the mayor of Whitehorn. It was an ugly scandal. Just before her death, Christina had given birth to a child. The baby girl had anonymously been left with her aunt. Rumor had it that Gavin, now out on bail, had killed his lover—Christina—to stop her from telling everyone he was the father. Most of the town had already tried and convicted him. Collin was sympathetic to the young doctor.

He glanced at Hope, a warning pinging along his nerves. A man could easily get in over his head when it came to dealing with a woman. He'd better remember that.

Hope kicked her foot free of the stirrup and gratefully slid from her mount. She stifled a groan and glanced around. After leaving Carey and Wayne and the children, she and Collin had ridden up a rough trail into the mining country of the old Baxter ranch.

The land, pitted with diggings, was dangerous because of the loose tailings that had been dumped by the careless miners of the last century. Some prospectors still roamed the area, she'd heard, in search of a lost sapphire mine.

The remains of a mining camp were evident in some one-room log structures, most without roofs.

She explored while Collin loosened the saddles and set the horses to grazing near a tiny creek. Both geldings drank thirstily.

She was ready for lunch. It was almost one, a good three hours since they had eaten the cinnamon rolls with Wayne and his family. She smiled, recalling Sophie's ambition to be a space adventurer and the girl's mother-hen bossiness toward her brother. Sophie took to the role of big sister with aplomb.

They were a nice family, Hope reflected. They had made her feel welcome.

Because of *him,* she added, watching as Collin laid out sandwiches and containers of spring water on a handy boulder.

"Ready?" he called.

"Yes." She joined him, sitting on a relatively flat rock with another behind ideally situated as a backrest. She grimaced as her tender rear came in contact with the stone.

Collin narrowed his eyes and studied her. He smiled suddenly. "Need a cushion?"

"Two of them." She grinned ruefully.

"How long has it been since you rode?"

She figured it out. "Since I was sixteen, I think. That's when I graduated from high school and stopped visiting a friend who had horses. I started college that summer."

"Hmm. You were pretty young. How long have

you been working for your father?" He handed her a sandwich and a bag of corn chips.

"Six years."

"Most people get their law degree when they're around twenty-five."

She was aware of the questions in his eyes. "If you're asking my age, I'm almost twenty-eight."

"A prodigy," he said "getting through college and law school at twenty-two."

"I was a good student," she admitted. "Not spectacular, but hardworking. Were you?"

"You don't want to know." He bit into his sandwich.

She followed suit, and they ate silently until curiosity overcame her. "You were an honor student," she said, blatantly fishing for information.

He burst into laughter. "I wish. English was my downfall." He shook his head. "All those essays on the dumbest subjects I'd ever heard of."

"Such as?"

"The social forms of the premodern, post-neoclassical period in English literature and art as compared with the postmodern, existentialist movement and confessional elements in twentieth-century novels."

She started laughing. "You're making that up."

"Well," he drawled, not denying it but not admitting to anything, either. He leaned close. "I like hearing your laughter. It opens up a whole new world."

Startled, she stared at him, the amusement dying

as she gazed into his eyes. Flames licked over her nerves at his intense perusal. Awareness flickered between them, as insistent as heat lightning in a summer storm.

With an effort, she looked away.

"It isn't going to disappear," he said, his voice rich with nuances that hinted at future bliss…and reckless, impossible complications.

She thought of pretending to not know what he meant, but discarded the notion. "Nothing is going to come of it," she said instead.

"Nothing?"

"No."

A wry smile curved his expressive lips in a self-mocking manner. "I hope like hell you're wrong," he said softly. "But I'm afraid you're right."

"We're enemies." She stated the fact bluntly.

"The lawsuit won't go on forever."

"For us, it will. The Baxters and the Kincaids will always be on opposite sides of the fence."

"That isn't true for all the Baxters and Kincaids, such as Brandon and Emma."

"Emma wasn't raised as a Baxter."

His expression hardened. "True, therefore she wasn't fed on hatred of the Kincaids from birth."

Hope surveyed the grandeur of the scenery. Hatred seemed terribly out of place here in this peaceful spot.

Sadness invaded her. She couldn't remember a

time when her father hadn't spoken of the Kincaids in derisive tones. It had been part of her life. But she couldn't honestly say she personally hated anyone.

"My father lost everything because of the Kincaids."

"He made a life for himself," Collin reminded her in gentler tones. "He earned a fortune on his own. He had a wife. And you."

Heat raced through her. His voice had dropped to a silken caress on the last two words. He made her feel as if she were a treasure beyond price, one that her father should have appreciated—

She stopped the wayward thought. "He lost his heritage, his rightful heritage, because of your family."

Collin acknowledged the thrust with a lift of his dark eyebrows and a shrug of his muscular shoulders. They finished the meal without further conversation.

He tilted his head toward the northwest. "There's a storm brewing. We'd better be heading back. You've seen the land Carey and Wayne have. It's rough and not good for ranching. This part is old mining country. Again, not good for ranching, but it's part of the Baxter holdings the trustees will sell you. We'll go to the northern section tomorrow."

"The one the tribal council bought?"

"Yes. The land is ideal for a resort there."

"And no good for ranching," she concluded.

He stood. "It has some pasture along the creek, but it's too damp for a housing development."

Stung by the implied criticism, she spoke sharply.

"Maybe my father wants to establish a family home and put down roots in the land of *his* ancestors the way your grandfather wants to do for his bastard grandsons."

"Is that what you want?" Collin demanded. "You're your father's only heir. Is that why you want the land?"

She didn't share her father's dream, but she'd never questioned his right to it. "I've never thought about it," she admitted.

He stood and gathered their debris. "You ought to think about what exactly you want for *your* future." He walked off and readied their mounts for the return trip.

Staring at his broad back as they rode single-file down the ridge to the valley, she wondered what she did want and why thinking about it made her ache inside.

Four

Garrett met them at the door when Hope and Collin arrived back at the ranch house. He was beaming. "I have a surprise for you," he told Hope.

For some reason she felt alarmed rather than pleased. Warily she followed the handsome older man into the family room or library or den or whatever they called it on a ranch. She recognized Emma Harper immediately.

"Emma, I want you to meet your cousin, Hope Baxter. Hope, your cousin Emma and one of my newest granddaughters-in-law." He was supremely pleased at the connection.

Hope smiled at the quiet, hazel-eyed waitress from the Hip Hop Café. At the time Emma had worked there, Hope had detected an aura of unhappiness around the young woman, but now there was a sweet glow in her eyes. Brandon, she noted, stayed close to his bride, as if guarding her.

"I've wanted to meet you," Hope said sincerely. "When I discovered you were a Baxter and we were kin, I was delighted." She gestured at the three men. "After all, we are seriously outnumbered by the Kincaids."

Brandon frowned, but Garrett and Collin burst into laughter at her little joke. Pleasure spread through her like butter on hot toast.

"I'm glad to meet you, too," Emma said, then looked surprised when Hope gave her an impulsive hug.

"Have a seat," Garrett invited. He served margaritas to everyone. Gina and Trent joined them. Trent put his son on the floor on top of the activity mat Gina had spread for him to play on. The men discussed ranch business.

To Hope, it was all very warm and homey. The way a family should be. She'd felt that familiar ache when Collin had told her about Wayne donating bone marrow to his little half sister. All the Kincaids seemed to share some kind of bond with each other. There was nothing like that among her family. Looking at the Kincaids gathered in the family room, she felt like a traitor in their midst, the spy who would use anything she heard against them.

"Did you know you have another Baxter cousin?"

Emma asked Hope during a pause in the conversation. "Rafe Rawlings was another child abandoned by Lexine. It's hard to believe that in addition to a twin, I've also had a half brother all these years."

"I've heard the rumors about the sheriff, but discounted it because of that Wolf Boy story about him being found in the woods and raised by a pack of wolves."

"Our dear mother left him in a cabin when he was only a toddler. I can only assume she was sure he would be found before he starved." She shook her head, clearly not sure Lexine had thought about it at all.

"Tangled webs," Hope murmured. "One act leads to another and our lives become hopelessly entangled."

"You have to wonder about that first rash act," Collin said, "the one that sets the whole chain of events in motion, especially in the case of murder."

"And once set, can anyone change the direction that fate seems determined to go?" Trent added.

"It takes courage to stand against the tide of opinion," Garrett mentioned. He turned a proud gaze on Brandon. "The way Brandon here did when everyone was sure Emma was the guilty party."

The young man looked embarrassed at the praise. "A person with one eye could see Emma wasn't the sort to hurt anyone. She didn't even know Christina Montgomery."

Emma laid her hand on his arm in a gesture of complete love and trust. Her eyes glowed happily as she gazed at her new husband. Hope was shocked at the sting of tears in her own eyes. She had that ache in her chest again, too.

Looking away, she encountered Collin. His gaze locked with hers and refused to let go. Flames danced in eyes that should have been as cool as a mountain lake but instead reminded her of lava stones, fresh from the fiery furnace of the life-giving earth.

She forced her gaze downward and stared at the refreshing drink in her hand. What Brandon and Emma had…it was never going to happen for her. She'd learned that lesson when her father had paid her sweetheart in law school to leave and never come back. He'd taken the twenty thousand and kept his word. She'd never seen him again.

Well, better to know sooner than later. But she'd loved him, or thought she had. She'd trusted him with all her heart. For a few short weeks she'd been dizzy with happiness. A sigh reached all the way to her soul. She'd never be that young and naive again.

"Dinner should be ready," Gina said. "I hope everyone likes beef stew."

"Supper, honey," Trent reminded her. "We're on the ranch now. We don't want to confuse the cowboys with city talk." He grinned at his grandfather and Collin.

"Impudent pup," Garrett muttered good-naturedly. He rose and extended his arm to Hope.

Confused, she stood. He tucked her hand into the crook of his elbow and escorted her to the dining room. Everyone got their own dishes and flatware from a sideboard. Trent brought in a crock of delicious-smelling stew while Gina carried the baby and placed him in a high chair. Emma and Brandon served hot bread and iced tea for those who wanted it. It was all very comfortable and easy.

"What do you contribute?" she asked Collin when he took a seat beside her.

He chuckled wickedly. "Didn't I tell you? We get to do the dishes. All by ourselves. Alone in the kitchen."

Heat rushed over her as the others laughed at the lecherous waggling of his eyebrows. She had to laugh, too. As the meal progressed, she had to admit she was having a good time. That worried her. A lot.

Hope found the kitchen was entirely modern. With a grin, Collin motioned her to a tall stool at a planning center and proceeded to load the dishwasher. Finishing the task, he started the machine, then washed out the slow-cooker and wiped up the counters.

"Done," he said.

She glanced at her watch. "In less than twenty minutes. I'm impressed."

"Let's take a walk."

She shook her head. "I have some papers I need to go over. I think I'll go to my room."

He shook his head. With a half smile on his face, he came toward her. He stopped a mere six inches away and laid his hands on the counter, trapping her within the frame of his masculine strength. His face loomed over hers.

She leaned against the counter, putting as much space as possible between them. The strange panic that had run through her the day of their meeting returned, stronger than before. She could feel it arcing from nerve to nerve until every part of her body was electrified.

"Don't," she said, a whisper of sound. She looked away from his compelling gaze.

"You looked scared," he said, puzzled. He crooked a finger under her chin, forcing her to meet his gaze. "I've never hurt a woman in my life. I don't intend to start with you. Especially with you," he added softly.

His breath touched her cheek. She felt hot, dizzy, confused by the panic. "I am scared. Th-this isn't good."

His half smile appeared briefly. "I think it would be very good. So do you. That's what scares you."

"No," she began, but couldn't continue the lie. "An involvement between us is out of the question."

"An involvement, yes."

His tone hinted at other possibilities that would be within the realm of acceptable. A shudder spread through her. He trailed his fingers down her throat, then settled both hands on her shoulders.

"What does the fight over the land have to do with us?"

She reared her head back. "Everything. Our families have been enemies for a long time."

He leaned closer. "I'm not your enemy."

"I won't be your lover."

She was appalled at the crass statement. It took all her control to maintain a level stare while waiting for him to tell her he hadn't asked her to be. He surprised her with a rueful smile.

"A man can dream."

He backed up a step, which allowed her to breathe a bit easier. She hopped off the stool. "I'm going to my room."

"It's still light. Let's go for a walk." He sliced her a sideways glance. "I'm restless."

The familiar heat seared along her veins, making her aware of the same restlessness within herself. When he started for the door without further argument, she followed more slowly.

Outside, the sun was setting. The sky was streaked with magenta and purple tones, spread with a lavish brush. The trees were silhouettes lined with gold as they climbed the lofty peaks surrounding the valley. Cattle and horses grazed peacefully in the pastures.

"It's so beautiful here, so…wild and free," she said, catching up with his long stride. She heard the longing in her voice and wished she could recall the words. They made her appear weak.

He stopped at the railing where horses once were tied when cowboys came in for a noonday meal or visitors rode over to chat awhile and leaned against it. He glanced at the scenery, then nodded. "It lets a soul breathe."

His words stirred chords in her. He understood what she felt. And that made him dangerous to her, more dangerous than the physical attraction they felt.

Yeah, right, soul mates, she mocked, trying to dispel the feeling. It refused to budge. A yearning for something she had never had gripped her. She couldn't even put a name to it. She clasped the wooden rail and tried to think.

Her father had told her she had to be careful, that men would want her for financial gain, not for herself, that people were not to be trusted. He'd been right.

She studied Collin. He had more reason than most to gain her favor. She had to remember that. He and Garrett wanted the lawsuit to end. Would they resort to any means to make that happen?

"A penny for them," he said, interrupting her endless circle of confusion.

"I was wondering to what lengths you would go to influence me in the case."

His wry laughter startled her. She turned a questioning gaze on him.

"Here I was thinking romantic thoughts of a twilight stroll and you're thinking of the lawsuit. Teaches me a lesson about my effect on the opposite sex."

"I won't fall for the infamous Kincaid charm," she told him, sounding stiff and priggish and stupid.

"No one has asked you to," he said in a tone of brushed steel. "You're right. Maybe you'd better go study your legal papers. You might find a loophole to oust the Kincaids from the entire county."

With that, he walked off into the shadows, leaving her to wrestle with regret and other emotions too turbulent to identify. The ache inside intensified. Retreating to her room, she acknowledged her instincts had been right, she shouldn't have come out to the ranch, but for different reasons than those connected to the lawsuit.

Collin Kincaid was dangerous to her peace of mind.

Hope groaned as she rolled out of bed shortly after dawn the next morning. Peeking out the window she saw others had been up for a while. Cade and Leanne were moving a string of horses from one pasture to another. Garrett and Trent, holding his son, were watching the animals as they went by, seemingly commenting on them.

She dressed quickly in a blue split skirt and white shirt and, unsure what to do, headed for the door. A note on the carpet told her to proceed to the kitchen. She studied Collin's neat handwriting, most of the letters printed the way engineers, accountants and those able to think down to the tiniest detail tended to do.

Hearing laughter in the kitchen, she hesitated before entering, then felt foolish as Emma caught sight of her.

"Come on in. We're just finishing breakfast. It's mine and Brandon's turn to cook. We've been arguing over sausage, eggs and gravy versus whole-grain cereal."

"Brandon and I won since we outnumbered Em,"

Collin spoke up. He was pouring orange juice into glasses that were already set on a tray.

"Next time I'm going to demand you be allowed a vote," Emma declared, placing a perfectly fried egg on a platter with several others. "Okay, let's go."

"Here, carry this," Collin ordered. He handed her a basket of biscuits while he carried the tray. "Good morning. Did you sleep well?" he asked on a deeper note when they were alone in the dining room.

"Yes, thank you." She placed the basket on the sideboard where jelly and homemade jam already waited.

Emma and Brandon followed with the rest of the food. Emma called down the hall to Gina. As if sensing a signal, Garrett and Trent and the baby returned to the house.

They sat down to the meal together. Garrett asked a blessing on all his family, those present and those absent. Then everyone filled his or her own plate with Hope going first, then Garrett.

Again she was reminded of how close the Kincaid family seemed to be and how different it was from her family.

Once she'd thought her father was the most wonderful person in the world. In her youth he'd taken her to the office with him. His staff had helped watch after her. It wasn't until she was older that she'd realized her sitters had left because he worked such long, unpredictable hours that they'd had no life of their own. So he'd taken her to work with him because he hadn't had a choice.

When had he become so obsessed with Whitehorn and his lost legacy there?

She realized it must have been in his mind for years. As soon as he started making a lot of money as a stock broker, then investment advisor, he'd started buying land.

"Do you like being a lawyer?" Emma asked, bringing Hope's thoughts back to the present.

"I really do," she admitted. "The law isn't perfect, sometimes it isn't even fair, but we have one of the best systems in the world for promoting justice for all."

"I'll second that," her new cousin agreed. "If it hadn't been for the law allowing additional DNA testing, I'm sure I wouldn't be here now."

Brandon looked fierce. "We would have found something else to clear you. That old prospector, Homer Gilmore, has been seeing aliens in the hills around here for years. It would have been his word against yours."

"Mr. Gilmore is a local. I was the stranger in town," she reminded him gently. She turned to Hope. "Brandon and his grandfather arranged for Elizabeth Gardener to defend me. She was wonderful."

"Did I tell you she's coming to visit us here at the ranch this week?" Garrett asked.

"Oh, it'll be so nice to see her," Emma said in delight. She touched Brandon's hand. "We're going to name our first child after her. If it's a girl."

"First child," Garrett repeated. His blue eyes—so very like Collin's, Hope noted—opened wide in pleasure. "Does that mean we're going to have a new grandbaby soon?"

"Yes, in about five months," Brandon admitted.

Trent picked up his orange juice glass. "A toast to the newest Kincaid."

Hope drank to the new baby, too. When she saw Collin watching her over the rim of his glass as he drank, she got flustered and nearly dropped the juice glass in her lap. His eyes crinkled lazily at the corners as he set his empty glass on the table. Her heartbeat quickened.

An hour later she climbed into the pickup and Collin started off across the pasture. At a gate— which he hopped out to open, then closed after they'd passed through—he pointed to a dirt road. "We'll be on a logging road. Rough, but better than your trying to sit a horse, I think."

At his knowing grin, she had to laugh. "I think I would have choked you if you'd brought out a horse this morning."

"Pretty stiff, huh?" He gave her a sideways glance. "You'll soon toughen up."

"I don't intend to."

"Hey, you can't live in ranching country and not be able to handle a day in the saddle. During roundup, we stay out in the hills for a week at a time. It's one of my favorite things—eating around a campfire, bedding the cattle down for the night, sleeping on the ground with nothing but stars between you and eternity."

"Mosquitoes nibbling at your nose, rocks digging into your back, snakes wanting to share your sleeping bag."

"Ah, you've done it, too," he said mock seriously.

"My father made me take a summer's survival course when I was sixteen. He thought I was too tenderhearted."

"Mmm, so that's what made you into the hard-nosed legal eagle you've become. I had wondered." He nodded wisely, then cut her a glance full of devilment.

She went all warm and smothery inside at his teasing. "Yes, I realized survival meant men, women and children had to look out for themselves. We were dropped in a wilderness area the last week. We had to eat off the land and make it back to base camp using the stars and local landmarks to guide us."

"It's more fun if you have a partner," he added softly, his gaze now bold as he perused her. "All life is. I realized that when I went to live with my granddad. He and my grandmother shared life in a way that was wonderful, not just for them, but for all of us around them."

Her heart contracted into a painful ball. "I wouldn't know about that," she said coolly. "My mother died shortly after I was born. It was only my father and me at home."

She held on to the seat belt as they bounced over the uneven road. The land was relatively level, but the road hadn't been graded that year. If ever, she added at a particularly bad pothole.

"This is the land that belongs to the reservation now," he pointed out after a full hour's ride over the vast ranch. "From here to the bluff where the creek runs."

"This was Baxter land?"

"Yes."

She opened the door when he stopped on a little rise and stood so she could see across the land. A rolling meadow bumped gently up against a rock wall. A line of cottonwoods indicated the meander of the creek.

"Can we get closer?"

"Yes," he said. "Get back in."

He drove across the meadow, startling a couple of deer lying in the tall grass, and parked in a shady spot near the creek. When she alighted from the truck, she could hear the sound of running water. The cool breath of mint mingled with the freshness of the breeze.

"Another beautiful spot. No wonder my father wants it." She picked her way around pines and firs mixed with the cottonwoods and willows until she stood on a boulder next to the rocky creek. She gazed farther down the stream. A line of rustic cabins made of split logs nestled on the other side of the creek in a tranquil, rather level, spot formed by a bend in the creek and the cliff, which descended to the valley floor and ended in a tumble of boulders that extended into the water.

"Oh, they're building," she said.

"The tribe has been busy this summer," Collin observed, stopping behind her. "They plan to put in several family resorts in order to bring in money and provide jobs. They're being very careful in using the land. Jackson Hawk has supervised several environmental studies. It's a reasonable use of the land that can be sustained without damage."

"Why can't this be used for cattle?"

"The pasture is too small for more than ten or so cow and calf pairs. Then there's the problem of transporting them out in the fall. The cows couldn't survive a winter out here on their own. Not enough forage."

"Oh."

He laid his hands on her shoulders. "Talk your father into settling for what the trustees can sell him. It's a fair offer."

Troubled, she twisted her head around and met his eyes. "It's his dream…" She lost the thought.

"Yes," he murmured. "Hope."

If he hadn't said her name, she might have been saved, but his voice, with that edge of tenderness and need… It was more than she could resist.

Tilting his head slightly, he bent toward her. She turned fully toward him and laid her hands against his chest. Heat immediately spread from him to her.

Neither spoke nor blinked for a minute, then he closed his eyes and his mouth touched hers.

It was bliss. It was the deepest pain she'd ever known. It was need and hunger and despair. It was excitement and guilt and all the things she'd ever experienced in this man's presence.

Tentatively, savoring the feel of his mouth, she explored his lips with hers, then with her tongue. A shuddering breath went through him. His arms wrapped around her, and she knew the meaning of cherished.

He was gentle and ardent at the same time.

It hurt way down deep inside—to know this and know it could never be. She turned her head. "No," she moaned. "Please...no."

Every muscle in his body tensed to the hardness of granite. He dropped his arms and stepped back. "Are you ready to go?"

She missed the teasing, the laughter in his eyes, the crinkles at the corners. She lowered her head and nodded. They made the trip back to the ranch headquarters in silence. When he parked, but before she could clamber down from the pickup, he touched her arm lightly then withdrew his hand.

"So, are we in agreement in trying to talk them into a settlement?"

She had thought about it on the agonizingly slow trip back. "Yes. I think it's a fair offer. I'll present it to my father and try to convince him to accept."

"Good."

"I think it's time for me to go home. I have contracts I need to go over before tomorrow."

But when she tried to start her car—a new one still under warranty—it wouldn't budge. A call to the dealer got her a promise to send out a tow truck the next day and haul it to the garage.

"I'll take you in the truck," Collin volunteered.

Having no choice, she followed him into the house to retrieve her overnight case. Inside she told everyone goodbye. She and Emma agreed to meet for lunch one day soon.

Collin drove to her condo at her direction. He carried her case inside, glanced around the living room, told her it was a nice place and left.

Later, having dinner—supper—by herself and gazing at the magnificent view from her window, she felt the silence of the mountains all the way to her soul.

She wished she dared accept the invitation in Collin's eyes. It would be foolish, yes, she knew that, but it would also be wonderful. She knew that, too.

And nothing could ever come of it.

No man would ever want her for herself. Her father had proven that to her. There was a sexual attraction between her and Collin, but nothing else. Their worlds were as far apart as the beautiful but lifeless moon from the earth. She had to accept that.

Get over it, she admonished herself. Don't get involved.

"The boy's in love," Garrett said to his houseguest.

Elizabeth Gardener, who had handled Emma's case at Garrett's request, smiled. "It happens."

Garrett turned from the scene outside where Trent and Collin were overhauling a tractor. He studied the lovely woman who was sixty-three to his seventy-three years. She was small, only five-four, with short, tousled hair that had once been blond but was now silver. Her eyes were blue and filled with lively intelligence. She flew her own plane to keep up with her busy schedule and was often a guest expert on "Larry King" and other such shows.

He felt a powerful stirring inside. "Even to old geezers sometimes."

"I don't see any old geezers," she told him smartly. "Only another of the handsome Kincaid men."

They looked at each other. She smiled. So did he. So, it happened, just like that, even to older couples, Garrett realized. But their futures would have to come later. There were other problems he needed her advice on.

"He can't have the girl, not with this suit between them. Maybe not then. Jordan Baxter hates us. It would take a strong woman to overcome that."

"Love can work miracles."

"I hate to see the boy get hurt. He once asked me if I thought he would turn out like his daddy. That sort of kicked me in my soul. I've often wondered how I failed my son."

"Sometimes it isn't our fault, the way our children turn out." She paused, then sighed. "Although I have to admit I blame Ellis Montgomery for Christina's sad life. The girl needed a strong, steady influence. Ellis left the home and child-rearing up to his wife.

When she died, Christina sought the attention she needed through unwise relationships."

"Her death, alone in the woods after giving birth, was a sad thing, a waste of a life. I'm not sure I've thanked you properly for defending Emma. She's become such a blessing in our lives." His eyes crinkled at the corners. "She and Brandon are expecting."

"That's wonderful. Grandchildren are the reward for being a parent. Wouldn't it be nice if we could skip right to that part without going through the torture of raising our own children first?" They chuckled companionably.

Garrett's thoughts returned to Collin. "Since we've been here in Whitehorn, Collin has mentioned that his dad and Jeremiah Kincaid were apparently cut from the same cloth. I think he's worried about himself as a husband and father and that he might be prone to the same reckless nature."

"What did you say?"

"I told him that good and evil existed in everyone and it's up to the person to bring out the best parts and to control the lesser facets of human nature. I told him he was a good man."

"He is. He's been extraordinarily kind to his newly found brothers. I find that admirable."

Garrett sighed. "But he's going to be hurt by that young lawyer gal."

"We all live through lost loves," she advised gently.

He nodded. "Your husband. My wife. It takes a while to get over it."

"Yes."

He looked at Elizabeth and thought of the years ahead. After a recent checkup, the doctor had joked that he'd likely live to a hundred. Twenty-seven years was a long time for a man to be alone.

"Elizabeth," he said slowly, "do you think you could see your way clear to living on a ranch? When you retire, of course. I wouldn't ask you to give up your work. You're too good at it."

She laughed. "I could be persuaded. Take me for a ride, Garrett, and fill my head with foolish notions."

"It would be a pleasure, ma'am, a pleasure indeed." His heart suddenly felt young.

Five

On Friday morning, after spending the earlier part of the week at the Elk Springs ranch, Collin parked the pickup under the shade of a cedar tree and walked over to the cabin where Wayne Kincaid was replacing a step to the front porch.

"Hey," Wayne called in greeting. His dog, Freeway, lying on the porch and keeping an eye out for rabbits and other intruders, wagged his tail lazily.

"Morning," Collin said, and ambled over to sit on the porch and scratch Freeway's ears.

Wayne's blond hair had a liberal sprinkling of white that gleamed in the morning sun, he noted. Freeway was getting pretty gray around the muzzle.

Time, thought Collin. He felt it slipping through his

fingers at an increasingly rapid pace. Used to dealing with time as seasons on the ranch, he wondered when he had become such an impatient person.

"What brings you over this way?" Wayne asked, giving him a shrewd glance.

"The damn lawsuit," he said in disgust. Settling it was the main thing on his mind. Baxter had refused their previous offer. The impatience rose in him again. "I've got a hard question to ask."

"Ask away." Wayne's expression was sympathetic.

He was another man, along with Trent, that Collin liked more and more as he got to know him better. "How hard would it be for you and Carey to give up this place?"

Wayne finished nailing the board into place, tested it with a tug to make sure it was secure, then sat on the new step before giving him a thoughtful frown. "Would it help get the suit settled if we did?"

Collin hadn't the foggiest idea. "It might. Jackson Hawk says the tribal elders aren't willing to give up the land they bought—they've started building cabins on part of it—but I thought I would try to get as much together as I could and see if Jordan Baxter would call off his dogs."

"Pretty nice-looking dog," Wayne commented, "that daughter of his."

Collin felt the heat hit his ears. Wayne grinned, then went serious. "Carey, Sophie and I have already discussed it. We'll let the whole place go for the same price the land was offered to your grandfather. If possible, see if you can cut out a five-acre site with the house for us. If Baxter won't accept that, then throw in the house."

Collin noticed two things while Wayne talked. One was that Wayne and Carey had included Sophie, Carey's daughter from her first marriage, in the discussion. That seemed fair since this was her home, too. And second, their total generosity as a family toward helping him settle the case.

"That's damn decent of you and your family."

Wayne swung the hammer idly. "Well, it was my father who did him wrong."

"You think Jeremiah pulled strings to get the loans called, as Baxter claims?"

"Given a choice in believing my dad and believing Jordan…yeah, I'd go with Jordan."

Collin thought of his own father. Larry probably hadn't been as conniving as Jeremiah, but Collin didn't think his father had been any more reliable as a parent. "It's a hard thing not to trust your own father. I hope I do better with my kids, assuming I ever have any."

Wayne's blue eyes—the Kincaid eyes—met his for a brief second of mutual understanding.

"I wondered about the same thing," Wayne admitted, his gaze on the far horizon. "Then I met Carey and Sophie. Amazing what a couple of females can do to a man's way of thinking. Of course, ol'

Freeway here was determined to stay, too. He fell hard for Sophie the first time they met. She shared her lunch with him and scratched his ears."

Collin chuckled. Sophie bossed Freeway around just as she did her little brother. "I agree with Freeway. That Sophie is hard to beat."

"I love her as if she were mine," Wayne said quietly. "She and her mother gave me a reason to live as well as to stay here in Whitehorn."

Collin knew Wayne had been a prisoner of war in 'Nam and had escaped with injuries so serious it was a miracle he made it back to the American lines. After he'd healed from the physical wounds, instead of returning to Whitehorn he'd drifted for years. The mental scars of hating his father had taken a lot longer to mend.

The companionable silence deepened between the men, then Collin got to his feet. "Thanks for your cooperation. Now to tackle Baxter again."

Wayne grinned. "Good luck."

Collin talked to Garrett about strategy later Friday afternoon. He explained his new plan for substituting the same amount of acreage sold to the Laughing Horse Reservation with good pasture from the Kincaid spread that adjoined the old Baxter property. That was as fair as they could get. Garrett agreed to the exchange. They called Ross Garrison, the attorney for Jenny and the trustees. They saw no problem with the idea.

Collin noticed his grandfather seemed restless, his mind on other things during the discussion. This was odd. The older man had been so concerned with the lawsuit and getting his grandsons settled, to the near exclusion of everything else for over a year.

"Anything else on your mind, G.P.?" Collin asked, reverting to his teenage habit of using the initials, which stood for *grandpa,* when he'd decided he was too grown up to use the kinship title.

"Huh? Oh…uh, no."

Collin's worry increased. "You aren't ill, are you?"

Garrett sighed, then smiled. "I'm fine, son." He paused, then asked, "What do you think of Elizabeth?"

Enlightenment came to Collin. "I think she's a fine woman and would be a great addition to the family."

To his delight, his grandfather blushed. "Well, I thought so myself," he said.

"Have you asked her?"

"Sort of."

"What did she 'sort of' reply?"

"She liked the idea of living on a ranch."

Collin let out a whoop and pounded his grandfather on the shoulder. "Wait till I tell the others," he said with a chortle, knowing his grandfather was in for some wicked kidding by the other grandsons.

"Keep it under your hat," Garrett ordered with a frown. His eyes were twinkling. "Let's get this mess solved first."

"I'll head into town as soon as I get showered."

* * *

Twilight was deepening the sky to gold and lavender as Collin drove through Whitehorn to the other side of town and parked in the guest parking lot at the condo complex where Hope lived.

He would invite her to dinner to discuss the new proposition. No Hip Hop tonight. They would have wine and candlelight out at one of the fancy tourist places on the main highway. Maybe they would go dancing later.

The blood surged hotly through his body at the thought of holding her. He wanted to do a lot more than that...

Okay, maybe they'd better not dance, or else she would accuse him of trying to seduce her to get her to agree to the new proposal. First he would get the agreement out of the way, then he would suggest dinner. Yeah, that would work. Then he could take her dancing.

Feeling better now that he had a plan, he marched up the sidewalk to her door and rang the bell. He admired the plants tastefully arranged around the small patio-like porch. Probably a gift from her friend— Meg somebody, the florist. And wedding planner.

Again his body reacted strongly to the thought.

Frowning, he rang the doorbell again and heard it chime within the condo. He peered at the window. A light was on inside, but he couldn't tell anything else as the shade was lowered to the sill.

"No one's home," a feminine voice said behind him.

He spun around. Hope stood there. His heart went into overdrive. She wore a sleek one-piece bathing suit with a towel draped around her shoulders. Her hair was wet and clung to her shoulders in curling tendrils.

Without makeup and her office uniform, she looked as delectable as the proverbial apple. Her skin was smooth and inviting. Her legs were long and shapely. Her hips curved seductively. Her breasts thrust against the suit top, the nipples visible against the material. Her lips were bare and soft and kissable. In other words, she was the epitome of the perfect woman.

"Hello," he drawled, stalling for time while he brought his body back under control. "I, uh, would you like to eat…go out to dinner…dance…"

His planned strategy evaporated from his memory and his tongue seemed equally determined to evade his mind's direction. "You're beautiful," he concluded.

She gave him a severe frown, which did nothing to dishearten his libido. "What are you doing here?"

"I, uh, came to talk to you. About a new proposal."

She unlocked the door and turned without inviting him inside. "What kind of proposal?" she asked warily.

His mind went completely blank. With an instinctive urge as old as mankind, he moved toward her. She moved back. He stepped forward again and realized he was inside. Some diabolical part of his brain took over. Without conscious thought, he closed the door behind him.

Her eyes opened wide, then narrowed on him. "Do come in," she invited in her precise back-East accent that could cut a man to shreds with little effort.

"Thanks. I will." He let his gaze run down her slender form all the way to her feet, which were narrow with short plump toes. The toenails were painted a pearly pink. To him, her feet looked delicate and tender. Perfect for her slim, graceful legs.

Every muscle in his body went into fight-or-flight mode—or making-love mode, whichever was appropriate.

"Dinner," he croaked, sounding like a dying man just crawling in from a trek in the desert.

"I haven't time."

He regained some control over his thinking processes. "There's a new proposal. About the land. It's a deal your father won't be able to refuse."

He groaned. He sounded like some actor from a B-movie.

"I need to shower and go over some papers."

Anger came to his rescue. "Then you refuse to take our offer to your client?" he demanded, reminding her of her legal obligations.

She opened her mouth, then snapped it shut. "Give me fifteen minutes." She walked off. "Make yourself at home," she called over her shoulder. "As I'm sure you will."

He grinned at her stiff back. "If I did that, honey, we'd be in bed."

Her chin sailed up in that haughty manner she could put on so easily. His grin widened as she refused to acknowledge the quip. Maybe it hadn't been wise, but it had gotten her attention. He heaved a deep breath and settled on the sofa to wait while she made herself beautiful. An unnecessary waste of time, in his opinion. She was already lovely beyond compare.

"What happened to your truck?" Hope asked when they reached his vehicle, aware of the man beside her in a thousand ways—all of them dangerous.

"I left it in Elk Springs." He cranked up the low, sleek sports car, a vintage model. "I found this old Corvette in a ravine out in the back country when I was boy. When I was a teenager, I got my grandfather to help me haul it out. I used all my ranch earnings to restore it."

"It's really lovely. You did a wonderful job."

"Thanks."

While his answer was sincere, she sensed his impatience with small talk. The air between them throbbed with unspoken questions, accusations… longings…

He took her to an expensive restaurant and presented her with the latest Kincaid plan. "Repeat that," Hope demanded, not sure she believed the offer.

"Wayne Kincaid will include his land in the sale, minus five acres with the cabin, if possible. If your father refuses to let the five acres go, then Wayne will release them, too. We can't do anything about the reservation land, but we'll throw in an equal acreage of prime pasture from the Kincaid land that joins the old Baxter land."

She mentally examined the offer from up and down, inside and out. "What's the catch?"

His grin crinkled the corners of his eyes. "No catch. The Kincaids are serious about settling this case. Are the Baxters?"

His startling blue eyes stared straight at her as he tossed the challenge at her feet. She mulled the settlement over. She had to admit it seemed like one her father couldn't refuse. "It seems fair."

"When will you present it to your father?"

"He's out of town again until Tuesday night."

Collin grimaced in impatience. "Call him."

Hope dug in her heels. Her father was handling other problems within the company. "I see no reason it can't wait. As you pointed out, it's been dragging on for a year. Another few days can't hurt."

He sighed and leaned back in the comfortable chair. Picking up his wineglass, he raised it toward her. "Here's to one more thing out of the way."

Hope lifted her glass. She looked a question his way as they clinked the crystal.

"Of us," he explained.

"There is no *us*," she snapped, sounding peevish, then was immediately angry with herself for showing that much emotion.

"There should be," he countered quietly.

Her heart lurched so painfully, she wondered if she were in danger of having a heart attack. She couldn't look away from his straightforward, level gaze. There was something in his eyes, something meant just for her…

With a final effort, she looked away and observed the other diners in the soft gloom of the candlelight.

"Coward," he said gently but with an edge.

"I'm not—"

"Yes."

She lifted her chin. This was ridiculous and she wasn't going to dignify the quarrel, or whatever it was, by arguing about it. Which made no sense at all. She absolutely and positively refused to verbally spar with him.

"Got it all figured out, counselor?" he asked lazily after a lengthy silence.

Giving him a glare, she replied that she did.

She repeated it to herself. She wasn't going to fall for the Kincaid charm, no matter that he made her heart go crazy with his lazy smiles, those delightful crinkles, that slow, burning way he had of looking at her as if she were manna from heaven and he wanted to devour her on the spot.

Heat flushed all over her body. A sheen of perspiration followed. Her pulse sounded in her ears like the plangent song of tom-toms beating on a distant shore.

"Stop," she heard herself say.

He understood the request. "Tell me how." His tone was wry, weary, ironic.

The music changed from soft background noise to a vibrant thrum. She realized a small combo had taken up position on a stage at the far end of the room. Couples rose at the invitation of the band leader and went to the dance floor. The lights dimmed even more.

It had been years since she'd danced, other than command performances at the company Christmas parties. Not since college had she danced just for the joy of it. Longing coursed through her. For a strange moment she wished she were back in those days when she'd been young and trusting, when she'd believed her heart.

But they were gone forever.

Tears misted her eyes, turning the candle glow into halos of light at each table. She blinked them away. "I need to go home."

"All right," he said as if sensing the desperation that overwhelmed her.

Outside, she filled her lungs with crisp night air that blew from the south, sweeping down from the Beartooth Pass, that heart-stopping gap through the mountain peaks that brought tourists from Yellowstone to Whitehorn. She felt she was at the crest of the pass, with that thousand-foot drop on each side. She only needed to take a step in either direction and she would fall…

No, no, no.

They reached her place all too soon. She had the car door open before he'd hardly turned off the engine. "I'll call you after I talk to my father," she said quickly.

He got out and met her on the sidewalk. "I'll walk you to your door."

"That isn't necessary."

Without replying, he fell into step beside her, his shoulder brushing her arm. It was like being burned whenever they touched. She could have wept.

"I feel so mixed up…" she started, then stopped, appalled at what her words revealed.

"It's tough," he agreed.

She was afraid to ask what he meant. At her door she put on a firm smile and held out her hand. "Thank you for dinner. It was lovely. I'll speak to my father Wednesday. I think this information is better delivered in person."

Collin took her hand in his and held it between his calloused palms. "I bow to your judgment," he said. A smile flickered briefly across his face, then disappeared.

She found she didn't want to break the contact between them. Gazing into his eyes, where the moonlight reflected a thousand dreams that equaled her own, she swallowed as misery rose in her. Her heart urged her to act, to take the moment and not look back. Her heart had been wrong before.

When he finally moved, she didn't protest. His arms gently circled her and his lips sought hers.

She raised her head and let it happen…wanted it to happen…*needed* it to happen….

She moved instinctively, wrapping her arms around his shoulders, feeling the soft fabric of his suit, sensing the controlled strength of his body.

His lips were sweet on hers and not at all impatient. He let the passion build through gentle pressure, then the softest forays of his tongue gliding along her lips.

When she opened her mouth to his caress, he leisurely accepted the invitation. Playful yet serious, he took possession, stroking along the edges of her teeth, finding her tongue and coaxing it into sensual play.

Her heart pounded fitfully and painfully. She finally turned her head, unable to bear more of his touch without coming apart. She wanted to weep, but couldn't. Inside, she sensed a powerful river of emotion push against the dam of hurtful past experience.

"Ambrosia," he whispered against her neck, laving her with hot moist kisses. "I think of holding you, kissing you, every waking moment. And in my dreams…" He lifted his head. "In my dreams, we don't stop at kisses."

His solemn perusal left it up to her. Without stopping to think, she removed the key ring from her purse and turned to the door. When she had it open, she stepped inside without flicking on a light.

Moonlight lay across the tiles of the entrance hall and living room like a silver path. She followed it. He followed behind her. When the door closed behind them and the lock clicked into place, his hands settled on her shoulders.

Hope leaned against him and let his warmth soak into her body. It was magic heat that warmed her all the way through, enveloping even that cold place deep inside that she hadn't been fully aware of. He moved around her and embraced her again.

His hands roamed her back and sides, seeking without demanding. She sighed and pulled his head down to hers until their lips melded once more. She couldn't get enough of his kisses and caresses.

"Collin," she whispered, needing to hear his name.

Collin fisted his hands in her hair and lifted handfuls of the fine material, letting it sift through his fingers. It was like water, like strands of silk, like magic.

The need pushed at him. "I want you," he told her, exposing the raw need, his voice hoarse with it.

"Yes," she said. "Yes."

She understood the yearning she heard in him, understood and responded helplessly to it, the longing great in her, too. With an instinct as old as the first man and first woman, she moved against him.

Collin ran his hands over her, experiencing the sweet flare of her curves with tactile pleasure. When his hands went to the zipper at the back of her modest black dinner dress, he moved slowly, waiting for the protest that didn't come. Relief flooded through him, adding to the harsh, hot surge of desire. He let off the control a bit as he slipped his hands inside the opening and explored tender flesh.

Hope caught her breath at the wonder of his touch, how gentle it was, how cherished she felt.

"You're warm and soft, like hot whipped cream," he whispered, pressing his face against the groove of her neck and shoulder and kissing her there.

With impatient, shaking fingers, she pushed at his jacket. He shrugged and it fell to the floor. She tackled his shirt. "Need to touch you…now."

Collin sucked in air and let her tug his shirt free of his dress slacks. He sensed her impatience. Elation added fuel to the flames licking through his veins.

Stepping back from her, he shucked his shirt, smiling at her little moan of distress when they parted. "I need you, too. Like water. Like air."

"Yes. It's so…necessary." And she realized it was, this need they shared. It was important, although she couldn't say how, or why, or when it had come about. "I don't understand—"

"Shh." He touched her lips with his, stopping any words of caution she might have uttered. He didn't want caution or questions between them. "It doesn't matter. Not tonight. Tonight there's only us. Everything else can wait."

"Yes."

And it was that simple, she found. To let go. To

dispense with clothing and inhibitions. To hold hands and walk side by side to her bedroom. To know his body.

"You're so incredibly gentle," she said almost on a sob as they lay together on the sheets, which felt cool beneath her.

"I want to be gentle with you," he murmured. "In ways I don't understand. Don't ever be afraid of me."

"No, of course not."

"I'd better take care of this." He held a foil packet in his hand. "Do I need it?"

"Yes. I'm not on anything. I haven't needed to be." Why was it so easy to be truthful with him?

"I bought these today," he said as his own confession that he hadn't needed protection in a long time, either. "I didn't know...but I'd hoped."

Only the briefest snatches of conversation were needed to explain. Her heart listened and filled in the spaces. She released a shaky breath and explored him fully. He did the same with her. When he touched her intimately, the playfulness disappeared, and they became all serious intent and urgency, all harsh demand and sweet giving.

When he rose over her, she met him eagerly. They merged, blended, became one.

"Collin," she said, suddenly frightened as a storm of emotion coursed through her along with the passion. "It's too strong...too much. Oh!"

He moved in her, hard and smooth. His mouth and

his hands caressed her in ways that intensified the longing and the panic. She clutched at him.

"Trust me," he said, feeling her fear as well as her hunger. He needed her trust as much as he needed the release in her body. More. It was necessary to his soul. "Trust me," he said again and heard the plea underlying the words.

She moved her head restlessly on the pillow, caught up in the throes of moonlight and luminescent fulfillment.

Thinking became impossible as his own climax poured over him, involving more than his body, taking him to places within himself that he'd never fully explored before.

"Heaven," he said a long time later when he could breathe easily again. He kissed the side of her mouth and rolled over, taking her with him, unable to give her up just yet. "Heaven and everything else."

He cupped her against his body, feeling the damp moisture of their passion, as tired as if he'd climbed a mountain in the brief hour just past.

"I think," he murmured, "that I've gone and fallen in love with you."

She looked as shocked as if he'd struck her.

Six

"No," Hope said miserably. "It's impossible."

"Difficult, not impossible," he said, running a soothing hand along her back. "The suit is all but over. Your father can't refuse to settle."

She had a feeling he could.

Collin must have read her mind. "If he does, we'll countersue."

"What basis?"

"Slap suit."

"How has my father harassed your family?"

"By refusing a reasonable offer, one some people might consider more than reasonable. Since land developers are known to use frivolous charges against others who oppose them, your father would be a prime suspect for using such tactics."

Tenderness was replaced by wariness in his eyes. She felt the loss deep inside. "Laws have been passed against that. The courts frown upon those who try it."

"Tell that to your father."

"If he loses, he'll be more than difficult."

Collin touched her cheek and ran a finger along her jaw to the corner of her mouth. "Let's not borrow trouble. We'll face whatever happens."

Together.

She heard the promise of the unspoken word. Warmth started in her heart and radiated outward until it joined the heat where their bodies touched. She pressed her face against his chest and kissed him through the wiry hairs.

Inhaling his scent, she marveled at his strength and his tenderness, at the fiery explosion of passion between them and how right it had felt. At last…she thought hazily as his hands grew more urgent upon her. At last, she was experiencing all of life.

"Collin," she murmured.

He was exploring her breast now and didn't raise his head. "Hmm?"

"Nothing. Just…it's more than I ever dreamed."

He looked at her then. For several heartbeats, for all of eternity. She felt her heart opening, slowly, like a door that hadn't been used in a long time. He smiled, his eyes gleaming in the soft glow of the table lamp.

"It'll be okay," he said. "I'll make it be."

When he dipped his head, she raised her lips to his and let trust come into her heart.

Hope frowned when she arrived at the office on Wednesday morning. Another car was in her usual parking space. She selected another spot, climbed briskly out with her briefcase in hand and headed for her office.

She had dressed with unusual care that morning. Her beige silk suit, with a smoky blue shell and blue and pink scarf, was one of her business uniforms, as Collin called them, but she felt feminine in it.

In fact, she felt feminine all the way to the core of her being for the first time in years. She knew why. Collin had spent the weekend with her. They had eaten and made love, swam and made love, watched old movies on TV and made love. He'd left early Monday morning to return to Elk Springs for meetings with the ranch foreman and some cattle buyers. He would return Friday.

Once she'd hated the weekend. She would rather be working than face forty-eight hours alone in her condo. Now she could hardly wait for the week to end.

Smiling, she entered her office.

"Your father would like to see you in his office," her secretary told her as soon as she stepped inside. Selma looked worried.

"Good morning, and thank you," Hope replied, unfazed. She knew her father and his moods. In her briefcase was the carefully worded settlement offer, composed by her and Collin over the weekend...when they'd had time.

Warmth tingled through her. Neither of them had mentioned love after his first shocking announcement, but the feeling had buzzed in the air around them, wrapping them in golden light and a thousand promises of the heart.

She tossed her purse onto the credenza, poured a cup of coffee, extracted the folder with the new proposal from the case and headed to the corner office.

"Go on in. He's waiting," her father's executive assistant informed her. A brisk woman with little time for small talk, she didn't commingle with the other workers.

Hope smiled her thanks. She entered her father's office with the smile still lingering on her mouth.

"About time," he greeted her.

She glanced at the designer clock on the wall. "I'm fifteen minutes early."

"I've been here since seven."

This was said in such a way as to imply she should have been in at that time, too. The familiar going-down-in-a-fast-elevator sensation attacked her. She had accepted long ago that she was never going to be able to please her father. She wasn't the son he'd wanted.

The warm glow of the weekend closed around her. She was fiercely, proudly glad to be female. Collin had made her feel perfect just as she was. She hadn't had to prove anything to him. She hadn't had to be witty or charming or anything. Only herself.

"Was there something you wanted to see me about?" she asked, taking a chair and setting her cup on the corner of his desk. She kept the folder in hand.

"What's happening on the case?"

She smiled as warmth stole over her. "I have some good news. The Kincaids brought us a new proposal."

Her father's eyes narrowed suspiciously. "What is it?"

She opened the folder and extracted the paper. After handing it to him, she settled back in the chair and sipped the mocha-flavored blend while waiting for him to finish reading the offer.

He snorted and threw the proposal onto the desk, then leaned back in the black leather executive chair and stared at her in disgust.

The tiniest qualm broke through the insulating glow that surrounded her. "The land being substituted for the property sold to the reservation is prime pasture with a year-round pond."

"It isn't Baxter land," he said coldly.

"It's equal acreage," she said, going quiet and still inside, the way she did when she'd evidently displeased her sire for no reason that she could discern. "It's a surprisingly generous offer."

His eyes narrowed. "Are you advising me to accept it?"

"As your attorney, I think it would be in your best interest—"

"Is that your considered opinion?"

She hesitated, a sense of danger striking a note of alarm in her. She studied her father, unable to fathom his mood. He appeared to be furious with her, yet there was a hard, triumphant gleam in his eyes.

"What are you upset about?" she finally asked.

He bounded out of the chair and leaned both hands on the protective glass covering the expensive desk. "Not a thing, other than my daughter carrying on like some empty-headed, love-struck teenager with the Kincaid grandson, that's all."

Hot words sprang to her lips in defense of the wonderful weekend she and Collin had shared. She would not let her father destroy the wonder of it for her. She retreated behind the icy calm she was able to summon when her father's anger threatened to overcome her.

"My private life has nothing to do with the offer being presented," she said.

He gave her a pitying look. "You're thinking with your heart, not your head. You let Kincaid get to you." He sighed. "I'd hoped to spare you this, but you leave me no choice."

Her heart rose to her throat. She swallowed painfully, not sure what was coming but knowing she wasn't going to like it.

He opened the entertainment center built into one wall and flicked a button on a tape recorder. Collin's voice came at her from the four speakers mounted behind decorative screens built into the walls.

"Yeah, she's gentling down real good," he said with wry humor in his tone.

"You think you'll have her under control before the big event? Otherwise I'll have to find something else."

"No problem," Collin assured his grandfather. "I have the touch. She'll come to my whistle before I'm through."

"Got her eating out of your hand, huh?" Garrett inquired skeptically.

"Naturally. Has the Kincaid charm ever failed?"

"Don't get too cocky, boy. You never know with females. She might decide to show you who's boss— Wait a minute. What?"

Hope heard Gina's voice in the background, then Garrett told his grandson, "Got to go. Finish up there and hurry back to Whitehorn before that little lawyer gal gets some fool notion in her head."

Collin laughed as if in delight. "She won't," he said confidently, his voice dropping to a lower note.

A frisson of pain shook through Hope. A sense of déjà vu left her disoriented as if time had somehow looped back and she was twenty again, staring at a canceled check for twenty thousand dollars and listening to her father tell her that her lover wouldn't be returning.

A thousand dollars for each year of her life, she recalled thinking at the time, that was what she had been worth. She took a deep breath and locked all feeling deep inside, then faced her father calmly.

"He was using you to get to me," Jordan said, fury darkening his face. "The Kincaids thought I'd change my mind if they could get you on their side."

"Then you decline the offer?" she asked, her voice level and devoid of emotion. "As your attorney, I must advise you that the courts may wonder why you would walk away from a settlement that is more than fair—"

"Fair!" he interrupted. "What's fair about being cheated out of your rightful inheritance by the trickery of the Kincaids? What's fair about using my own flesh and blood for their ends? They're all bastards, if you ask me, no matter which side of the blanket they were born on. Don't you see that, or are you too starstruck at having one of the mighty Kincaids wine and dine you?"

She suddenly knew who had informed her father of the weekend spent with Collin. That weasel, Kurt Peters.

"No," she said quietly, "I'm not starstruck."

Her father paused in his tirade and studied her. He came around the desk, sat on the arm of her chair and laid a hand on her shoulder.

"I'm sorry, bumpkins. I never meant for you to be hurt or to have to learn a lesson the hard way in dealing with the Kincaids. They stoop to anything to get their way."

His sudden kindness and the use of the childhood nickname—earned for her breakneck pace of rushing into things as a child—nearly broke through the reserve she'd erected around her emotions.

She laid her cheek against his hand for a second, then straightened. "Shall I tell Garrett you decline the offer?"

"I'll call the old buzzard and tell him myself. The Baxters aren't dead meat yet."

Hope smiled grimly at her father's words. "I'll handle it. It's my job." She rose and, taking her cup and folder with her, walked to the door. "By the way, that was obviously a taped telephone conversation between Collin and his grandfather. You might remind Kurt it's against the law to tap people's lines without a court order. All the lawyers in the world won't be able to keep him—and you—out of prison if you're caught."

Her father had the grace to look uncomfortable. "At least we know Kurt is on our side. You would go far before you found another man as smart and loyal."

She returned his gaze levelly. "Loyal to whom?" she asked softly before opening the door and departing.

Walking down the tastefully carpeted hallway, she contemplated her parting shot to her father. She didn't trust her father's right-hand man. Kurt made her uneasy with his watchful eyes, his cunning and ambition.

But then, she had been wrong about two men in her life, both of whom she had trusted. The pain went deep, but she couldn't think about it now. She had work to do. Grateful for the mind-absorbing details of the law, she entered her office, secure behind her icy shell.

Selma shot her a sympathetic glance. Hope smiled to dispel the worry in the other woman, then went into her office and closed the door.

A few minutes later she left word at the Kincaid ranch for Collin to call her at his earliest convenience. When she hung up, she stared out the window at the mountains.

Now what?

"Now we wait," she said to the empty room, and refused to think of lies and deception, of trust and sharing. She pressed her hands tightly together as if by doing so she could hold fast to the dream.

But it had already flown.

Collin stared at the brief letter, typed on expensive letterhead from the Baxter Development Corporation and signed by Hope with her title, Corporate Attorney, under her name. He swore as he glared at her neat signature.

"I can't believe he turned it down," he said to his grandfather. "It doesn't make a lick of sense. The man is crazy. He ought to be locked up."

Garrett nodded, his expression also angry.

Collin pushed the breakfast plate back and crossed his arms on the table. It was Friday. He'd gotten up in the wee hours of the morning, anxious to get back to Whitehorn to see Hope.

His heart bucked around in his chest like a rodeo bronco in the national championships. He'd planned on going to her place as soon as he got in, but his grandfather had been up, eating a solitary breakfast when he arrived.

Collin had cooked up some sausage and eggs and joined the old man. When he'd asked what was wrong, Garrett had shown him the letter.

"I'll call Hope and find out what's going on," he promised, eager to do it. He needed to hear her voice, that sweet way she said his name.

His body went into red alert.

With an effort, he controlled the hunger and focused on the difficulties presented by her father. The man had to be certifiably insane—

His grandfather let out a heavy sigh. Collin studied the older man. For the first time that Collin could ever recall, Garrett looked tired, almost defeated.

Damn Baxter and his lawsuit. This wasn't a dream; it was an obsession.

"Elizabeth been up this week?" Collin asked to distract the old man.

No brightness entered Garrett's eyes. He wasn't to be diverted this morning. "She flew in Wednesday for a half day. What do you think Baxter will accept?"

"Nothing less than all the Kincaids being drawn and quartered and deposited outside Montana, preferably in grizzly country to finish off the pieces," Collin replied, unable to keep the bitterness hidden.

Garrett gave him a quick glance. "This going to interfere with your plans for the little lawyer gal?" he asked, quick to discern his grandson's concern.

"Not if I can help it." Collin heaved a deep breath. "I'll call her and find out what's the problem. The man can't refuse our offer just like that." He snapped his fingers. "He's crazy."

Growing more furious with Jordan Baxter the more he thought about the letter, he filled his coffee cup and went to the office.

He called Hope at her apartment but got her answering machine. "Hello. Are you at the office already? All work and no play," he scolded, then spoiled it by laughing. "I'm back in Whitehorn. Drove half the night to get here. I'll see you at your office around ten. If you're in the shower…"

Pausing, he thought of last weekend and all the things they'd shared, including the shower. Heat ran rampant over his body. He pushed the images aside with difficulty.

"…call me as soon as you can."

For the next three hours he stayed close to a telephone, expecting her call at any moment. At ninethirty he drove into town and parked in front of the impressive headquarters of Baxter Development.

"She's not available," the secretary told him when he arrived at her office.

He studied the woman's bland smile. "Is that the truth?" he finally asked. "I need to talk to her."

"Truly, she's in a meeting with Mr. Baxter. She'll be tied up most of the day."

He mentally cursed, but managed a smile for the woman. "Tell her to call me when she gets a moment. Here's my cell phone number." He scribbled it on a notepad on the desk and left the building, although not without a strong urge to search every room until he found Hope.

A sense of disaster loomed over him. He had a feeling he needed to talk to Hope right away. Quelling the impatience, he stopped by the sheriff's department to see one of the deputies, Sterling McCallum.

"Come in," Sterling invited. Sterling and his wife had adopted Jenny as a baby before learning the girl was Jeremiah's child. Sterling was the main trustee of the Kincaid ranch for his daughter. He removed some folders from a chair and indicated Collin should be seated.

Collin showed him the letter.

"The man's crazy," Sterling said with a frown, handing the letter back. "I can't believe any court would back up his claim against our offer."

"I'll follow up and find out what the problem is," Collin promised grimly. "Or else I'll just shoot him and get this over with."

Sterling's smile was wry. "Better let the law handle it," he advised. "*I'll* shoot him."

They discussed the next step, which was a court hearing a couple of months away. Ross Garrison, the ranch attorney, and Elizabeth Gardener were consulting on the case. While Elizabeth specialized in criminal law, she was an expert trial attorney and was advising Ross on the presentation of their facts to the court.

At eleven-thirty Collin returned to Hope's office. Her door was closed. "They're having lunch sent in," the poker-faced secretary told him.

He stared at the closed door to Hope's inner sanctum. Without explaining his action, he walked over and thrust the door open. The office was empty.

His ears hot, he turned back to the openmouthed secretary, muttered "Thanks" and walked out before he made a bigger fool of himself.

He called and left word on her office line, then twice more on her home phone, reminding her to call as soon as possible. He waited until midnight before going to bed.

Saturday was a frustrating repeat of the previous day as far as talking to Hope was concerned. So was Sunday. She didn't return his calls, which admittedly were growing angrier in tone as he left messages for her. He was aware of Garrett's worry and was grateful that his grandfather didn't question him.

Sunday evening, Collin drove into Whitehorn. He went by Hope's place, but she didn't answer the door. Driving back through town, he spotted her car on the main street. He whipped into a parking space and headed for the café. The Hip Hop was one of the few places open on Sunday.

Sure enough, she was there, having dinner with her friend, the wedding planner. Meg's little boy was seated in a high chair between the two women.

"Mind if I join you?" he asked, then took a chair without waiting for a response.

"Not at all. Collin, right?" Meg inquired with a welcoming smile and a quick glance at Hope.

"Right." He turned to Hope. "Hello."

His voice came out husky, a spoken caress. He watched her eyes flicker to his, then away. Yeah, she was avoiding him. Anger gnawed at his control.

"I guess you've been too busy to answer my calls," he mentioned casually, giving her a chance to explain.

Her lips thinned and her chin tilted up. "Didn't you get my letter?"

"The one refusing our offer? Yeah. It didn't make a lot of sense. We need to talk about it. Now or later?" He glanced at Meg, who pretended not to listen as she spooned green peas onto her son's plate.

"There's nothing to discuss. The letter was self-explanatory."

He didn't think there was anything about her he could dislike, but that precise, distant New Yorker tone nearly made him lose his cool. He wanted to shake her and dislodge that cloak of icy control. He wanted to know what the hell was wrong, why she'd changed from one weekend to the next.

The waitress came to take his order. "Cheeseburger with everything. Iced tea," he said. She left quickly, as if sensing the tension at the table.

"Well," he drawled, putting a twist of humor on the word, "I'm kinda dense. Maybe you'd better spell it out."

"My father didn't accept the offer."

"And that's that?"

"Yes."

He took a deep breath. "What happened to the warm, sweet woman I held in my arms last Sunday?" he asked.

The blood rose fast and furious in her face. She stared at him aghast. Then her face closed once more. "She learned not to be a fool for the legendary Kincaid charm."

"Which tells me exactly nothing," he snapped in frustration. "Explain that."

Several heads swiveled in their direction. Meg was listening openly now. Even Gabe was watching him warily as he stuffed a pea into his mouth. Collin leaned forward and stared into Hope's blue-gray eyes. It was like staring into a smoky veil. Gone were the warm depths he'd wanted to dive into and never come up.

"Call my office tomorrow for an appointment if you wish a meeting on the case," she said. "Shall I invite my father to attend?"

"You can invite your father to go to hell. What's happened between us?"

"There is no—"

He pushed his chair back. It screeched across the floor like a scalded cat. Silence fell around them. He was aware of breathing hard, as if he were swimming for all he was worth against an invisible tide that was sucking him in, pulling him into a whirlpool…

"Tell your *client* we'll see him in court." Collin put a sneer on the word, threw a twenty on the table and walked out before he did something he would regret—like kiss the devil out of her until she confessed she was as crazy about him as he was about her.

Exercising all his control, he drove out of town at only slightly above the speed limit. But at the ranch he saddled up a mean gelding and rode hell-bent-for-leather until both he and the horse were too tired to fight each other.

It wasn't the weekend he'd envisioned.

Seven

"Tell her I want an appointment. Today."

Hope shook her head at Selma.

"Uh, just a moment, please," her secretary requested of the angry man on other end of the line.

"I'm not in to him."

"I'm sorry, Mr. Kincaid, but Miss Baxter is tied up all day," Selma reported to Collin.

"Fine. Tell her I'll be at her office at six o'clock. Be there or else!"

Hope didn't need for Selma to repeat the message. She'd heard his angry voice from three feet away. She smiled with forced calm at Selma's wide-eyed look. "I guess I'll have to meet with him and get it over with."

She returned to her office, but hiding in the details of the law didn't work for her today. It hadn't worked over the weekend, either. After seeing Collin at the Hip Hop, she'd been hopelessly caught up in the memories of their weekend together.

Her heart lurched painfully. The tears she'd refused to shed since hearing the tape rose perilously close to the surface, making her head feel stuffy, as if she had a cold.

Had it ever been said: love hurts?

Only in every mournful cowboy song she'd ever heard since moving West, she answered, cloaking her heart in cynical humor. At twenty she'd been devastated at the loss of her first love, but not now. She knew the heart did indeed go on. She'd learned, oh, yes, she learned...

Forcing herself to concentrate, she went on the Internet and researched precedents where land cases, mostly involving the early railroads, had been over-turned by the courts due to fraud. By sheer dint of will, she managed to get through the afternoon.

At five-thirty, she cleared her desk and locked the file cabinet. At five minutes before six, she paced the carpet, her palms sweaty, her fingers displaying a telltale tremor as she waited for Collin. A light knock on the door sent her heart to her throat.

She cleared her voice and said, "Come in."

Kurt smiled as he entered. "About done? Jordan suggested we run through the details of the case. I thought we might have dinner and discuss it. If you wish," he added as an afterthought.

Resentment flared. Her wishes counted for nothing. Both of them knew it. Her father wanted Kurt to check out the legal arguments she planned to use.

"I'm busy tonight." She glanced at her watch. Two minutes before six. She checked the street in front of the building. No sign of Collin yet.

Kurt looked disappointed. "We could have a late dinner," he suggested.

"I don't know how long I'll be."

"Another time then." He lingered near the door. "What do you think about the Nighthawk trial? It looks pretty bad for the Indian, doesn't it?"

"Yes." Hope didn't think Kurt was interested in Gavin Nighthawk and his problems. He wanted to know who she was meeting. So he could report to her father? She shrugged. "I don't think the doctor is capable of cold-blooded murder. Of course, if Christina Montgomery threatened to expose him as the father of her baby… People do strange things when they're cornered."

The baby, Alyssa, now lived with her aunt, Rachel Montgomery, who was married to Jack Henderson, private investigator and brother to Gina Henderson, who was married to Trent Remmington.

Tangled webs? Snarled beyond redemption was more like it. And the Kincaids were in every loop and knot.

A movement in the street caught her eye. Collin slammed the door of his pickup and was heading up the sidewalk.

"So that's who you're waiting for," Kurt said.

She whirled. He was standing right behind her. His blue eyes glinted with anger, then it was gone.

"He wanted to discuss the case."

"Didn't you send him the letter refusing the offer, as Jordan instructed?"

The resentment flared again. "Since my father has apparently discussed it in detail with you, I'll leave it to you to figure it out," she said coldly. "Now, if you don't mind, I have an appointment."

A vein pounded in his temple, but Kurt smiled in his ingratiating manner and headed for the door just as a sharp rap sounded on it. "Come in," he invited, opening the door to Collin. "She's expecting you."

Hope suppressed a strong urge to throw a crystal vase at the back of his insolent head. "Collin," she said in acknowledgment of his presence when they were alone.

"Yeah, your archenemy."

A flush spread swiftly over her cheeks. "Please say whatever is on your mind. It's been a long day."

"I agree." He tossed his hat onto a hook on the antique lowboy and pulled a chair to the side of her desk. "I want to know what's happened to turn you into a harpy. And don't give me some cock-and-bull story. I think I deserve the truth from you."

She remained standing behind her desk, but it didn't feel like a power position. She sat and pulled her chair closer to the desk. She didn't face him, but stared at the expensive walnut surface as if studying the wood grain was her top priority at the moment.

"Well?" he demanded.

"Last weekend was a mistake. I failed to keep a proper distance between my job and my…emotions."

"Oh, hell," he muttered. "Spare me the dissertation. Why was it a mistake?"

She glared at him. "Because we're enemies. We're going to be facing each other in court in a couple of months."

"That has nothing to do with us."

"It has everything to do with us. I'm a Baxter. You're a Kincaid. I was foolish, letting myself succumb to a moment of insanity."

Her chest ached as if her heart had swollen too large for her body to hold. She pressed a hand between her breasts and saw his gaze follow the movement. Heat and humiliation pounded through her.

"How easy you must have thought it was, to sweep me off my feet. The famous Kincaid charm—"

"That's the second time you've mentioned the Kincaid charm and accused me of using it on you. Exactly how did I do this?"

"You know," she accused, meeting his frosty-blue gaze stoically. "When you told your grandfather—"

Too late she realized where her tongue was taking her.

"Told my grandfather what, exactly?"

She licked her lips, stalling for time. She knew he wouldn't quit until he found out what he wanted to know. "That you had me eating out of your hand."

He frowned, looking more puzzled than angry. "When did I say this? And how did you hear it?"

Should she say she eavesdropped the weekend she spent at the ranch? "It doesn't matter."

"The hell it doesn't," he said, softly menacing as he leaned forward. "I never said any such thing to my grandfather or anyone else. I especially wouldn't say it about you."

She couldn't bear for him to lie. "You did. I heard you—"

"How?"

"On the tape my father— On the tape someone gave my father."

His nostrils flared at the mention of a tape. "I want to hear this tape."

"No."

"Yes." His tone was softer yet. Dangerous. "If I have to tear this building apart, I'll find it. Shall I start in here or in your father's office?"

Something in her expression must have given her away.

"Ah, your father's office. Of course."

When he stood, she did, too. She caught his arm.

"I'll play the tape for you. If you try to use it in court against my father, I'll bring up the fact that you were in collusion with your grandfather to destroy our case."

There was a tense silence.

"Did our weekend mean so little to you that you would use it like that?" he finally asked.

"Did it mean anything to you?" she countered.

He watched her without saying anything for a long moment, then he gave a snort of bitter laughter. "How can I answer when everything I say is used against me?" He opened the door. "The tape," he reminded her.

Her back stiff, she led the way to her father's office. Using her key, she unlocked the door and opened the entertainment center. The tape was still in the player. She clicked it on.

Collin's and Garrett's voices filled the office. When it ended, she rewound it and turned the machine off. To her amazement, Collin started laughing.

Only icy control allowed her to bear it without screaming or hitting him with the nearest object, which happened to be one of her father's prized Remmington bronzes. She wouldn't give him the satisfaction of watching her lose control.

"So that's what this is all about," he said when she closed the cabinet. He came toward her. "Honey, that wasn't about you. I'm training a filly for my sister. It's a gift from Granddad for her birthday." He stopped in front of her. "The tape is doctored. More than one conversation was put together to form it. That last part was from an earlier conversation, long before our weekend, and concerned a change of venue motion. My grandfather thought you might ask for one."

"Would that be a problem for him?"

"Not at all. Just an inconvenience."

He looked so earnest, his manner open and honest. She pressed fingertips to her temples where a headache pounded as furiously as her heart. She wanted to believe Collin…. No, that was foolish.

Her father hadn't lied to her about the love of her young life while she was in college. He wouldn't lie now. He had no need to. Collin had every reason to gain her trust—

"You don't believe me," he said incredulously, breaking into the rapid-fire thoughts filling her mind.

"My father wouldn't lie," she began, then stopped at the fury that flashed over his handsome features.

"But a Kincaid would?"

She had no answer. A battle raged inside her—her father on one side, Collin on the other.

"I don't know," she whispered miserably. "The tape… Are you denying it's your voice?"

"No, only that the context is different from the original. I would never deceive you."

His tone dropped, becoming low, sexy, intimate. The way it had been when they had made love.

"Hope," he murmured.

When he moved a step toward her, ready to touch her, she instinctively stepped out of reach. He went as still as stone, then dropped his hands.

They stood two feet apart while a mile-deep chasm opened between them. From the street came the honk of a horn, an impatient blare from one weary driver to another. From overhead a plane droned, taking tourists on a jaunt to the awesome Beartooth peaks. Within the building, silence reigned except for the occasional clink of a wastebasket being emptied.

"All right," he finally said, and walked out.

She watched from the window as he strode to his truck. He stopped and gazed up at her office. She stayed hidden behind the miniblinds until he climbed in and drove off toward the Crazies to the northwest of town.

When he was gone, she sank into the chair. The quiet slithered into her and emptiness surrounded her, as if she had moved into a vacuum. The loneliness came from inside her, as if everything had fled, even her heart. There was nothing left except the necessity of keeping up the facade of living.

She clenched her hands tightly together and felt the beat of time echo in the empty corridors of her soul. After a few minutes she forced herself to move, to gather her purse and briefcase and go home.

"I really appreciate your coming over," Meg said, dashing around the cottage in a dither.

"You know I love keeping Gabe," Hope assured her friend. "He's my favorite fellow. Aren't you, handsome?" she asked the child, who was splashing happily in the tub.

"No," he said with a smile.

"He's already entered the Terrible Twos. *No* is his favorite word."

Hope laughed at Meg's exaggerated grimace. "Okay, big boy, time to get out before you turn into a prune. We're going to read the story about Spot and the circus."

"Spot!" Gabe shouted. "Spot!" He splashed water in Hope's face as he stood and threw his arms upward for her to lift him from the bathtub.

"I won't be gone long," Meg promised. "I only have to arrange the baskets at the reception, then I'm done."

"No problem. Take your time."

Meg dashed out of the cottage, leaving Hope to care for Gabe.

Hope was secretly thrilled at the trust her friend showed in her by asking her help. She dried the toddler and after some maneuvering got him tucked into his pajamas.

Sitting in the rocker in the nursery, she read two, then three of his favorite books, which she had let him pick out. He fell asleep during the last one.

Tenderness rose in a vast wave of longing as she carried him to the crib. His head lolled against her shoulder. He turned his face into her neck. His

sweet baby scent filled her nostrils. She wished…
She wished…

She held her breath as emotion, hot and urgent,
beat at the walls of her control. A second passed, then
another. She pressed her lips together hard, but it
was no use.

The tears, the useless, ridiculous tears, came,
falling upon Gabe's feather-soft hair and running
into the tender folds of his neck. Once started, they
wouldn't stop.

Cuddling Gabe's warmth to her, she wept silently
for all the things missing from her life—a home,
children of her own, a loving mate….

When Gabe stirred in her arms, she carefully put
him down and raised the side of the crib. She laid a
thin blanket over him and turned out the light.

From the hall, she detoured into the bathroom
and splashed water on her face. Looking at her reflection, she was shocked at how wretched she
looked. There were circles under her eyes and lines
where she didn't remember having any before. She
felt old and used up, as if all her youthful vitality had
drained away.

For the first time, she realized, she had no hopes,
no expectations that life was going to be any different or any better from what it was at this moment.
Some vital part of her had given up on dreams.

She sighed shakily and dried her face, refusing to
dwell on a future that appeared very bleak. It never

did any good to cry or to obsess over what might have been. She'd learned that long ago at her father's knee.

Thinking of her father, she returned to the living room with its vibrant array of plants and flowers. Rummaging in her briefcase, she pulled out her opening argument and went over it, word by word. Kate Randall Walker would probably be the judge in the case of *Baxter versus Kincaid et al.* Hope had to have all her facts and precedents readily at hand. Kate wasn't known as the "hangin' judge" for no reason.

Meg smiled as she watched the bride and groom circle the reception, thanking their guests for coming and making each person feel welcome. The baskets of "wild" flowers—cultivated and grown for this purpose—looked lovely, if she did say so herself. She was finished and could go home, but something caused her to linger.

Hope, she thought. Her friend was her usual smiling self and yet...

Meg shook her head, a sense of Hope's unhappiness haunting her. There was something between Hope and Collin Kincaid and it was a lot more than Hope was telling. Just how involved were they?

Sex?

There was definitely a sizzle between them. Meg didn't know how far it had gone. Hope and Collin were mature and attractive people.

Love?

Maybe.

But it was never going to have a chance to grow and develop, the way things stood between the families.

In her car, Meg started the engine, and for one moment hesitated before putting the car in gear and driving off. Instead of turning toward her cottage, she drove south of town. She knew Jordan had a home bordering the new golfing community Baxter Development had built. She was going to stick her nose in somebody else's business, but so what? All he could do was whack it off.

On this wry note, she turned into the impressive driveway and parked on the circular drive in front of the house. Lights were on. He must be home.

She hopped out and rang the doorbell before her courage ran out. She'd just decided to leave when the door swung open. A scowling face greeted her. Jordan's eyes took on a puzzled expression as he gazed past her as if to see if Hope was also there.

"Hello," she said more cordially and calmly than she felt. "Uh, may I come in?"

Her words seemed to prod him into graciousness. "Of course," he said. He peered behind her into the night. "Are you alone?"

"Yes. Hope is staying with Gabe. My little boy," she added. "I had a wedding reception to cover tonight. My assistant was busy."

She realized she was chattering and shut up. Anger

overcame the case of nerves as she recalled Hope's eyes while the younger woman bathed Gabe. Such despair in her friend, and this man was the cause, or at least a good part of it. She squared her shoulders.

"I was just relaxing in the library. Join me," Jordan invited. He gestured for her to come in.

Meg had been in elegant homes. She'd seen gilt and marble and fine art tastefully displayed. But she'd never been in Jordan Baxter's home. "This is lovely," she said sincerely, gazing at floor-to-ceiling bookcases.

"It's a replica of one my wife did for me when we lived in New York. She had excellent taste."

"Exquisite," Meg agreed.

The oak floors gleamed. An Oriental rug of ruby red and a soft misty shade of green on a golden-beige background outlined a conversation grouping of morocco chairs and sofas. Black granite, glinting with golden flecks, detailed the fireplace and a desktop. It was repeated in pedestals that supported American West art pieces.

"What would you like to drink? Brandy? Sherry? Wine?"

"Sherry," she said.

He brought the drink to her in a stemmed ruby-colored glass. A pattern of flowers and vines was hand-cut into the crystal so that the leaves and petals were clear glass. She studied it appreciatively before taking a sip.

"Very good," she murmured.

His smile was dry. "What brings you to my humble abode at this time of night?"

"Your daughter."

The smile disappeared. "Hope," he said, a note of disapproval—or disappointment?—in his voice.

Meg resented the tone. "Hope is one of the smartest, most honorable people I've ever met. She's also loving and kind. And desperately unhappy."

Jordan's expression hardened. "She has reason to be unhappy," was his reply.

"Because of Collin Kincaid, yes. But he isn't the direct cause. You are."

"I'm sure I don't know what you're talking about. Or that it concerns me." He lifted a brandy snifter and swirled the liquor, his manner cold and distant.

Meg sipped the sherry and thought of the desolation in Hope's eyes. "So you care nothing for your daughter's happiness, or that your obsession with revenge on the Kincaids is destroying her life."

"Destroying her life? A bit dramatic, wouldn't you say?"

"No," she said staunchly. "She's in love with Collin, or she could be, but she can't acknowledge it because of you. Because of her loyalty to you."

He flashed her a furious glance. "My daughter might have been overwhelmed by the Kincaid charm, but she isn't in love with the Kincaid grandson. As for revenge, as you so succinctly describe it, my *case* against the Kincaid trustees really isn't any of your business."

"I know," she admitted. "I came here on an impulse that I'll probably regret tomorrow. But I don't at this moment." She gave him a challenging grin.

He looked taken aback.

"Hope told me something of what was going on with your suit after the local TV news reported on the Nighthawk case developments. You're using Hope for your own purposes. She's caught between her love for you and her love for Collin—"

"She is not in love with Kincaid!" Jordan broke in, his temper boiling over.

"She is," Meg insisted. "If you'd accept the settlement the Kincaids offered, she could admit it. That would remove the first obstacle, I think."

"I won't settle for less than what I was supposed to get before old Jeremiah cheated me out of my inheritance."

Meg's shoulders slumped. She rose. "Well, it was a long shot, but I'd hoped you would see reason. I'm going to encourage Hope to listen to her heart," she said, being totally honest with him, "because I think you're wrong. The Kincaids seem to be offering a fair deal. You're the one being stubborn."

"Who are you to talk to me this way?" he demanded, his eyes like stainless-steel daggers.

"No one," she admitted. "Absolutely no one you need concern yourself about. But I am your daughter's friend," she couldn't help but add as a parting shot.

She walked out of the house, her head high, leaving him standing in his magnificent library, aware that he was alone with all his wealthy surroundings, caught up in the past and the disappointments of his youth. She felt sorry for him.

But more so for Hope, who was paying the higher price for his lost dreams.

Meg frowned all the way home, her thoughts going at a furious pace. There must be some way she could help her friend. And maybe Jordan, too. He had to get over his obsession with revenge. For his own as well as Hope's sake.

Thinking of a parent's duty to a child, she sighed as guilt ate at her. She had her own problems along those lines. She knew Garrett was looking for a seventh grandson, the last bastard child sired by his son, Larry.

Furthermore, she knew Gina had traced Larry's whereabouts to Whitehorn at the time the child was conceived. Why had Larry left that letter to indicate the possibility of another child?

That child did exist. Gabe. Her son.

She had deliberately slept with Larry Kincaid—though that wasn't the name he'd used at the time—because she'd wanted a child and considered the handsome but shallow stranger the perfect sperm donor. He wouldn't bother her asserting his rights as a father since he plainly didn't care about anything but the pleasure of the moment.

That had suited her at the time. But now…what was fair to Gabe?

She didn't want to lose her child, and she was afraid that could happen if she went to Garrett and confessed. He might go to court for custody. With the Kincaid money and influence, things might not go well for her.

Sighing, she had to admit to a tiny bit of admiration for Jordan in that he dared to take on the whole clan. She hadn't summoned that much courage yet. The Kincaids were a formidable force in the state.

However, Collin seemed a very decent person. She'd seen caring in his eyes when he gazed at Hope. Anger, too, but that was justified in light of Hope's refusal to see him again after that torrid weekend.

Reading between the lines when Hope alluded to the brief interlude with the rancher, Meg had concluded things were quite involved between them. The couple had shared more than a few hot kisses.

Ah, to be young and in love and miserable and elated and all those things that went with falling totally in love.

She laughed as she parked under the carport at the cottage. Right. She was so old and experienced at these things. Going inside, she found Hope as she'd expected—diligently going over her legal notes.

Looking at her friend's reddened eyes, Meg resolved again to try to help, even if she did get her nose whacked off in the process. "How was Gabe?" she asked.

"A doll as usual," Hope replied brightly. "You should be grateful to have such a perfect child."

"I am," Meg said on a thoughtful note, a little ripple of fear going through her. "I truly am."

"Meg…"

"Yes?" When Hope hesitated, Meg urged her to speak her mind. "Ask me anything. I'll answer honestly."

"Did you love Gabe's father very much?"

It wasn't the question Meg had expected. She gazed solemnly at Hope. "I didn't love him at all. In fact, I hardly knew him. I wanted a baby."

Hope stared, wide-eyed.

"Yes, I know. It was probably foolish of me, but I was over thirty, with my own business and money in the bank. I could support myself and a child."

"What are you going to tell Gabe when he's older?"

"The truth—that his father did me a favor."

"What if the man returns?"

"He won't. He died shortly after our, uh, interlude. I thought at the time it simplified things. Now I'm not so sure." Her shrug was rueful. "Well, we all live with our decisions, wise or not."

"Yes," Hope agreed.

"You'll have your family someday," Meg assured her friend for no reason except she'd always believed goodness should be rewarded just for being.

Hope shook her head. She smiled, but it was sad and resigned and hopeless. "Not me," she said.

"Listen to your heart," Meg advised, and wasn't at all sure which of the two of them she meant.

Eight

"Into the lion's den," Collin remarked to Garrett.

His grandfather's wry smile reflected the way he felt upon arriving at the Baxter Development Corporation's offices. Ross Garrison, their attorney, pulled into a parking space next to them.

Wayne Kincaid and Sterling McCallum were next. Clint Calloway was the last of their group. The three men, along with the attorney, were trustees of the Kincaid holdings for Jenny McCallum.

Wayne, the legitimate son, and Clint, another Kincaid bastard, were entitled to part of their father's wealth, but both men had declined, wanting nothing from a man who had never been a decent parent to either of them. Or to little Jenny, their half sister, whom the whole town doted on. The kid was a trooper.

What a messy lot humans were, Collin thought as the men greeted each other and headed for the conference room where Baxter and his attorney had agreed to meet with them. Face-to-face, his grandfather thought they could get Jordan to agree to a settlement. Collin had his doubts.

Jordan's secretary met them in the impressive lobby with its native plants and Western art. "This way," she invited pleasantly, and led them to the elevator and the conference room on the executive floor.

All was quiet elegance up there. Mahogany Row, as some employees called it, was an appropriate term. Gleaming wood, expensive carpet, gilt lettering on each corporate officer's door. No raised voices. Very impressive, Collin scoffed.

They were shown into the conference room and served coffee by the secretary. She offered various pastries, which everyone declined, then left them.

A minute later the door opened. Collin's heart went into overdrive. Jordan entered first, the leading point of a triangle with Hope and another guy flanking him.

"Gentlemen," Jordan said by way of greeting. He didn't offer to shake hands but went to the head of the gleaming table immediately. Hope sat to his right. The other attorney, Kurt somebody, Collin vaguely recalled, took the chair to the left.

"Morning, Baxter," Garrett said affably. "I think you know everyone on this end of the table. I don't know the young fella with you, though."

"Kurt Peters, my attorney...one of my attorneys," he corrected with a glance at his daughter.

Anger spread through Collin at the slight to Hope. She was the primary attorney on the case and had done most of the work. He quelled the impulse to say something to this effect and let his gaze feast upon the woman who'd occupied all his dreams and much of his waking thoughts of late.

She wore a gray suit with a blue-gray blouse that crisscrossed over her breasts. A simple gold chain and gold earrings were her only jewelry besides an expensive watch that had probably cost as much as his pickup. A gift from her father, no doubt.

Looking beyond her icy calm, he noted circles under her eyes and two tiny frown lines over the bridge of her nose that makeup didn't quite conceal. She'd been burning the midnight oil.

A picture of her dressed in nothing but a smile and a towel wrapped around her hair came to him. He nearly groaned out loud and thought of cold things— icebergs, the Arctic, the river in springtime.

Her smoky gaze met his.

For a second he saw, or imagined he saw, yearning and loneliness mixed in those depths. Then it was gone. She nodded without smiling and looked back at her papers. Their weekend might never have been.

Recalling the hours of their intense lovemaking nearly made him groan a second time. She'd been a perfect lover—passionate and responsive, innovative and playful. He witnessed no traces of that woman in the attorney facing him across the chasm of the conference table. That fact caused a strange ache to echo inside him. He forcefully shut off the feeling and concentrated on the problems at hand.

"Since I called the meeting," Garrett said, "I'll start. I guess I want to know why you refused our offer," he said directly to Jordan. "What exactly is it that you want?"

"My rightful inheritance, nothing more, nothing less," Jordan told him with cool disdain.

Garrett studied his opponent for a long moment. "We basically offered you that. You refused it."

Jordan's smile was thin. "The cliff property wasn't included."

Collin saw the tensing of a muscle in his grandfather's jaw, but Garrett smiled again, affably and with a touch of irony, as he held his temper.

"Son, we can't give you what isn't ours to give," the older man explained. "The trustees here have agreed to include a like acreage that adjoins the old Baxter place. It's a better piece of land—"

"Says you," Jordan interrupted. "But that cliff face might prove to have gold or something of more value."

Garrett looked perplexed. "There's never been any

gold found in the creek that runs along there. I don't see what else…ah, sapphires."

"Maybe," was all Jordan would say.

Sterling McCallum spoke up. "Both the Kincaid and Baxter places have been prospected for over a century. There once was a sapphire mine, but it played out. A new vein was found a few years ago, but it was insignificant. If there's anything of value left, it's hidden well beyond modern methods of finding it."

"Be that as it may," Jordan said, "I still intend to have the original deeded land. I don't think the mighty Kincaids have enough influence in the state to block my acquiring it, considering that I'm willing to pay more. I've put my original offer in writing. Your attorney should receive it tomorrow at the latest."

He flicked a glance at Ross, then looked back at Garrett. His smile said he'd covered all bases and there was nothing Garrett could do. Collin wanted to knock the smile, along with the man's teeth, down his throat.

Looking at Hope, he controlled his temper. She could have been made of stone for all the emotion she displayed. A feeling that he should do something drastic came over him. It had nothing to do with the land.

Hope needed rescuing.

It was that simple. And that complex. He had a feeling she would turn to stone if he didn't get her away from her father and his unreasonable hatred of all that was Kincaid-related.

"What a waste," he muttered into the silence.

Several pairs of eyes bore into him, including smoky blue-gray ones that hadn't looked icy at all when they'd made love. Despair cast gloom into his soul.

"A waste of time," he added, looking at Hope, then at his grandfather. "He doesn't want to settle. He wants to harass us. I say we countersue."

"On what grounds?" Kurt Peters inquired smoothly.

Collin looked at Hope.

"Slap suit," she answered when the silence stretched to several seconds.

Kurt raised his eyebrows derisively. "You would have to prove intent on our client's part."

"That should be easy enough," Collin told him.

He didn't mention the illegal wiretapping. That had been a disclosure from Hope to him. He wouldn't use it unless he had to. He glanced at her and saw she understood.

Jordan laughed and spoke to Garrett. "Your bastard grandsons will all be old men before they can legally live on the Kincaid place. If ever. Maybe you can arrange to have them buried there," he said, his smile coldly victorious.

Garrett stood. "I'm sorry, men," he said to his group. "I can see I've wasted your time in bringing you here." He stared at Jordan down the long, gleaming table. "I thought face-to-face we could make sense of this mess and come to a reasonable agreement. But one has to deal with reasonable men in order to do that."

Collin was proud of his granddad. His tone was as cool and scornful as Baxter's had been. Baxter flushed a dark, angry red.

Ross spoke to Hope. "You should have a serious talk with your client. Our efforts at settlement won't go unnoticed by any court in the state."

"Don't be surprised if the case is tried outside Montana and out of the jurisdiction of Kate Randall Walker and the rest of your cronies," Kurt told them contemptuously.

Wayne Kincaid looked murderous. Kate and her husband Ethan were longtime personal friends of his. Sterling and Clint moved closer to him as if they thought they might have to restrain him from charging down the table and strangling the obnoxious attorney.

Hope, Collin noted, seemed appalled at the insult. She met his eyes and quickly gazed at the folder on the table in front of her. He saw her hand tighten on the folder, but she said nothing.

The hunger rose in him, physical, yes, but there were other elements, too. Again he sensed desperate need and knew it came from her, although she sat perfectly calm and still.

Instinct urged him to grab her and run, to save her from some unseen danger.

When he tore his glance away, he found her father's gaze on him. The man had gray eyes, similar to Hope's, but there was nothing soft in them. Collin returned the hard stare. Baxter looked away first. When Garrett rose, Collin did, too.

"There's nothing more to say," his grandfather stated, and turned to leave.

Walking to the door, Collin held it open for Garrett and the rest of their party to exit. He paused before following them. "I'll see you after the trial," he said to Hope, determined it would be so.

"No," she said, that stricken, panicked look returning to her eyes.

Again he felt she needed rescuing. From her father? Or herself? Collin didn't know, but he knew what had to be. He smiled grimly. "Yes."

Then he left quickly before he yanked her right from under her father's nose and took off to the high country where no one would find them for months.

Jordan would probably shoot him in the back if he tried it. His oily attorney Kurt would help. What would Hope do?

Joining Garrett at the truck, he admitted his didn't know.

"It'll work out," Garrett said suddenly as Collin backed out of the parking space. "Life has a way of working out, son."

"Yeah," Collin said, feeling the way he had at fourteen when he'd been sick at heart for the cool mountain valleys of Montana and his grandfather, the one person he knew he could count on. "Yeah," he said again and sighed.

* * *

Collin became aware of someone approaching from the house. He glanced at the darkening sky and realized he'd been standing for some time with his arms on the top rail of the paddock, watching the mares that had been sold and were to be picked up in a day or two by the buyer.

"Hey," Trent said to let him know who he was.

Collin moved over a bit, giving his half brother room at the corner of the fence. Trent joined him in leaning on the top rail.

"It must be hard to sell an animal when you've watched or even helped it being born," he commented.

"It's part of ranch life you learn to accept early on," Collin told him. "It's worse when you lose one to lightning or an illness you couldn't cure or didn't notice in time."

They stood there in companionable silence while the moon rose over the far hills.

"Don't let her get away," Trent finally said.

Collin didn't pretend to ignorance. "She doesn't trust me. I can't change that."

"Hmm. The way I figure it, you got to hang in there until you change her mind."

"Is that what you did with Gina?" Collin kept his tone light, but he was intensely interested in the answer.

"Yeah. It wasn't easy. Hard-boiled detectives are nearly as hard to crack as hard-nosed lawyers. Know what you mean?"

"Uh-huh," was all Collin would commit to.

Trent chuckled, then became serious. "Don't give up without a fight, bro."

"Then you think I should, uh, pursue the matter?"

"That's up to you and how serious you feel about the situation. And the woman."

"I feel like kidnapping her," he admitted, "but that probably isn't good form in this day and age."

"Probably not. Try talking a lot. Women like that. Of course she'll say no to whatever you say. That's when you kidnap her and head for the hills."

Giving Collin a cuff on his shoulder, Trent ambled back toward the house. He'd no sooner disappeared than another shadow emerged from the stable. His grandfather took Trent's place at the fence.

"I settled many a question in my mind by leaning on a fence and watching cows or horses," he said.

"Yeah? You going to give me the benefit of your life experiences, too?" Collin asked cynically.

Garrett grinned. "Is that what Trent was doing?"

"Yeah. He told me to talk to Hope, then kidnap her."

The older man snorted with laughter. "A good thinker, that boy. Are you going to follow his advice?"

"I don't know." Collin sighed, feeling gloomier than the shadows cast by the craggy peaks around them. "I don't know how to save a person from herself."

"She'll have to come to her own conclusions," Garrett agreed. "But that little lawyer gal is smart. She knows what's what. She'll come to her senses."

Collin wondered if that was true. Or if he was the one who needed to face facts.

"But it can't hurt if you use a little friendly persuading, can it?" his grandfather continued, giving him a sly smile. "I don't let Elizabeth get too far away before I call and remind her I'm around and plan to be for a long time. I'm going down to see her in a couple of days."

"You think I should go see Hope?" Collin asked, not at all sure this was the thing to do.

"Yes," Garrett said simply and, with a smile, walked on to the ranch house.

Brandon was next.

"You got some advice for me, too?" Collin asked with more than a smidgen of irony.

Brandon scowled, but his reply was friendly enough. "Not really." He gazed into the starry sky as if searching for a navigation point. "But Baxters and Kincaids can be more than enemies, if both of you set your minds to it."

With that sage remark, he walked off, heading back to the wife whose side he rarely left these days.

Collin stalked over to his truck, got in and revved up the engine. He yanked it into gear and shot off down the road before Cade, Blake, Gina, Emma or someone else in the growing Kincaid clan decided to offer an opinion on his love life.

His frown eased as he considered how he felt about Hope Baxter. Worry and tenderness edged out despair and anger. It was asking a lot of a woman to want her to deny her closest relative, the father who had raised her, and come to him.

But that's what he wanted—her love and trust. A future. And children. They could have a good life in Elk Springs. The town needed a sharp district attorney. And he needed a wife. She was the only one who would do.

It was that simple.

Hope showered after her swim, then prowled through the condo, straightening pictures on the wall, rearranging her few personal belongings in the condo. Some of the pieces were antiques, inherited from her mother's New England ancestors, who'd been ship's captains first, then captains of industry later.

However most of the furniture had been selected by the decorator hired by her father. Hope had been indifferent when she'd bought the model home, complete with furnishings. She'd just wanted a place of her own, a sanctuary to run to.

That thought disturbed her, and she shied from it as a picture of the Kincaid ranch came to her. Occupied mostly by men, the ranch house still managed to convey an air of comfort and ease. Even the Native artifacts, all museum quality and displayed in glass cases along the hallway wall, seemed ready to be used.

By contrast, the Western art her father favored

somehow seemed contrived on its expensive pedestals. She shook her head at the disloyal thought while worry ate at her.

Pulling a jacket around her shoulders, she left the condo and chose the path around the tiny lake in the complex. Her thoughts returned to the case as always.

She thought her father was wrong not to take the Kincaid settlement. They'd had words about it after Garrett and his group had left the conference room that morning.

Kurt had backed Jordan. No surprise there. He agreed with whatever pleased his boss. Disgust filled her, and she realized how much she despised the other attorney.

And this was the man her father would have her become seriously interested in.

She stopped on the far side of the lake and watched the sliver of moon rise over the crags between Whitehorn and the Beartooth Pass. The wildness, the pure vastness, of the land flooded her heart. She pressed a hand to her chest as pain and longing erupted from a pit deep inside her.

She wished she had never moved to Montana. She wished she'd never heard of Whitehorn or the Kincaids...

Liar, the trees murmured. The wind whispered the word back to her. She lowered her head as tears, hot and unexpected, burned behind her eyes. She hurried back to her condo as if a pack of wolves nipped at her heels.

"Hope," a voice said out of the dark.

She started as a dark form separated itself from the shadows near her door. Her heart nearly leaped from her body. "Collin," she said on a gasp.

"Sorry, I didn't mean to startle you."

He shrugged, a restless movement of his broad shoulders. She saw he wore no jacket. The night air was chilly. She pulled her coat more tightly around her.

"What are you doing here?" She made no move to unlock the door. She didn't want to invite him inside.

Again he shrugged, a dark shadow against other shadows. She had a feeling of unreality, as if each of them were specters who had chanced to meet on their nightly prowl. They stood there for an eternity, both silent, waiting for the other to move.

The wind caressed her neck with chill fingers. She shivered, then strode forward, stepping past his dark shape, careful that no part of her touched any part of him. When she unlocked the door, she heard his footfall, then felt his presence as an absence of the insistent night wind on her neck and down her back.

"I want to come in," he murmured.

"Why?"

"To talk."

His voice had dropped to a husky whisper, and again the pain and longing swept through her like a tidal wave. "No," she said. "There's nothing to say."

His ironic laugh brushed her temple when she

glanced over her shoulder at him. "Then let's not talk," he said.

Before she could do more than blink, his hands clasped her shoulders, turning her. She opened her mouth—to protest?—but his mouth touched hers just then.

The hunger drove all coherent thoughts from her. With a low moan, she clutched his shirt and pulled him closer. She closed her eyes, blocking guilt, regret and other warnings from her conscience as she savored the feel of warm lips on hers.

The kiss and the questions it asked—and the answers it found—went on for a long time.

When they came up for air, she said, "If this is wrong…" she paused to search for words to complete the half-expressed wish that something could make it right, but none came.

"It isn't," he told her. He lifted her, stepped forward and kicked the door closed behind them. Then his mouth was there again, seeking, demanding, giving….

His lips left hers and roamed her face and throat, leaving a hot trail that caused shivers whenever he moved from one spot to another. His hands wandered over her back, then slipped under her sweatshirt, creating lava flows of yearning that rippled outward from every place he touched.

She shifted restlessly. He touched her breast and the ache centered there. But it was ecstasy, too, and that's what she didn't understand. What was it about this man, this one man out of hundreds she had met, that stirred her so?

He caressed her until she was dizzy with hunger. Against her abdomen, she was aware of the hot tumescent need in him. She could fulfill that need and find the answer to her own wild longing with him.

"You can make me think the impossible is reasonable," she said on a half laugh of despair, planting kisses along the base of his throat and down the vee of his shirt, knowing whatever was between them was never going to be fulfilled.

"Anything is possible," he assured her.

Sorrow tempered the excitement of being in his arms and experiencing the raw perfection of his kisses. The chasm between them was too wide, too deep. He refused to see it.

Tenderness, the most dangerous of all emotions, swept over her. She touched his face with her eyes closed, memorizing him through her touch.

"Bliss," he murmured, his mouth rapacious against hers, "The greatest bliss...touching you..."

"Yes," she agreed, sounding breathless and all too eager, ready to be swept away. "But it's wrong..."

"No." He raised his head and glared at her. "Everything else in our lives is off kilter, but not this. This is the one thing that's right."

"How can it be?" she asked, sanity returning in a cold steadying wave of painful frustration. "We're on different sides. There will always be a gulf between us."

"I've missed you," he said, ignoring her logic. "Come away with me. Come live with me."

Longing was a separate pain in each part of her. "I can't. Please, don't ask impossible things."

Desolation replaced the passion of a moment ago when his arms fell to his sides. Anger mixed equally with the hot desire in his eyes. She knew which she wanted to encourage.

He leaned close without touching her and spoke. "I was wrong when I said I thought I was falling in love with you—"

Her heart gave a frantic lurch.

"—I am in love with you. For what it's worth."

She turned from him, needing time to absorb this new declaration. Picking her jacket up from the floor, unaware of when it had fallen, she looked at it helplessly, then tossed it onto a chair instead of hanging it in the closet as she usually did.

She sat on the sofa and cupped her hands around her elbows. Feeling betrayed by her body and its demands and by the yearning to take what Collin so generously offered, she sighed at the irony of the situation.

"It's impossible. My father…the case…"

"I'm not your enemy," he said softly, his eyes hot, angry and hungry…gentle and tender.

"Sometimes I think I'm my own worst enemy," she said with a brief, bitter laugh.

"The lawsuit has nothing to do with us—"

She stared at him as if he was out of his mind.

He smiled slightly. "It has to do with land and old hurts and dreams that can never be recaptured. Jeremiah Kincaid is dead. Your father has no real quarrel with my grandfather. We have as much right to buy the land as anyone. When this case is over and forgotten, you and I will still exist."

"And we'll still be enemies. You say the tapes I heard were doctored. I asked. My father says they're not."

Fury blazed in Collin's eyes, but his voice was quiet when he said, "So it comes down to my word against his. Who are you going to believe?"

She met his probing gaze and realized how a witness must feel being questioned by a hostile prosecutor. "M-my father." The tiny stutter gave away doubts she couldn't let herself express.

His gaze softened. "In the end, you'll come to me."

"I can't," she whispered, closing her eyes against the hot masculine appeal of him. When she looked at him, she saw strength, honor and steadfastness, all the things a woman wanted in a mate. An illusion. She'd learned that years ago.

"I'll wait," he promised just as softly.

She heard the door open and close. When she looked, he was gone. She touched her lips, the moments in his arms already seeming more a dream than reality.

The night closed around her and still she sat,

huddled on the sofa as if afraid to move, as if she would fall into a million pieces if she did.

The moon rose higher. Its light through the window formed a rectangle on the carpet. She looked out and saw a star hanging low in the sky. "Star light, star bright," she said.

She wished…she wished…she wished she had never met Collin Kincaid.

Liar, the night wind whispered.

Nine

Meg listened. Yes, there it was again. Someone was knocking at the door. She glanced at Gabe, happily splashing in the tub. "You expecting company?" she asked.

"No," he said as he did to every question nowadays, then giggled as he squirted himself in the face when he squeezed his rubber duck.

"I didn't think so. Who is it?" she called down the hall. She had no time for guests. Unless it was Hope. Her best friend was always welcome.

"Jordan," replied a masculine voice.

Her mouth dropped open.

"Jordan Baxter."

"That's who I thought you meant," she said but to herself as her heart hopped around like mad.

Grabbing a towel, she swept Gabe up without warning. He screamed in fury at being taken from his bath. Ignoring him, Meg rushed to the door and opened it. "Is anything wrong? Hope? Has she been in an accident?"

Jordan's smile was ironic. "No to all the above. May I come in?"

"Of course." They had to speak loudly due to the screaming Gabe. Meg stepped back and tried to smile. "He doesn't like being taken from his bath. It's his favorite playtime."

"So put him back in," Jordan suggested.

Meg considered. "I'll put on some coffee first—"

The crying toddler was taken from her arms. Both she and Gabe shut up as Jordan tucked the boy against his shoulder, folded the towel more securely around the naked little body, then headed down the hall.

"I think I remember how to do this." He grinned at the gaping Meg over his shoulder. "I raised Hope, you know."

Meg recovered her poise. "She's a wonderful person, but I think she raised herself."

With that parting shot, she went into the cozy kitchen and put on a pot of decaffeinated coffee. When it was brewing, she returned to the bathroom. Jordan was seated on the commode beside the tub.

He was telling a complicated story of a sea rescue involving Rubber Ducky of the Fire-and-Water Rescue Squad. He directed Gabe in squirting water on a "burning" boat. She watched silently until the story was finished, then gave her son a two-minute warning that bath time would soon be over.

When she announced time was up, Jordan again surprised her by lifting Gabe out and drying him off before turning the child over to her for tooth-brushing.

"Has he any more teeth yet?" Jordan asked. "Hope said you were getting worried about that."

"Yes, he has several now. They all came through at once. He drove me crazy chewing on everything. It was worse than having a puppy."

When Jordan laughed, she did, too. And that surprised her—that she was laughing with this man she disliked for his insensitive treatment of his daughter.

"What are you doing here?" she asked while Gabe rinsed his mouth with a lot of noisy spitting.

"Damned if I know," Jordan said.

That was the truth. He didn't know why he'd stopped here at this tiny cottage that would fit inside his library and entrance hall. He followed Meg as she went into the boy's bedroom and watched as she tucked her son into pajamas. She glanced at him, her eyes frankly perplexed, but settled into a rocking chair and proceeded to read a story.

The child nearly fell asleep and made no protest when she laid him in the crib. Something caught in

Jordan's chest when she bent forward and kissed her son.

The boy—Gabe, that was his name—grabbed his mother's hair and pulled her forward until they rubbed noses, then he grinned and closed his eyes as he yawned, the picture of a tired but happy child after a busy day of discovery in a safe and wonderful world.

Jordan swallowed against a tightness in his throat. He vividly recalled Hope as a baby. She'd wanted no one but him to tuck her in at night and had screamed until he'd rocked her and sang silly songs so she could go to sleep.

A long time ago. A long, long time…

Meg motioned him to follow her. She closed the door and led the way down the hall to the kitchen. "Would you like a piece of pineapple upside-down cake?" she asked politely.

An impulse, too strong to ignore, came over him. Like the one that had prompted him to stop at her cottage. He shook his head and moved forward. Her eyes opened wide in shock as he bent to her mouth. "This will do," he said huskily and kissed her.

He felt the tremor run through her. He thought it was from her, but it could have been from him. He didn't know and suddenly he didn't care.

The kiss deepened as she responded instead of shoving him away and socking him as he'd half expected. He slid his arms around her as her tongue met his in a sweet caress, and stepped closer, gathering her in and experiencing her warmth all the way down his chest, abdomen and thighs.

He shuddered as hunger washed through him. She rubbed his shoulders, then his neck and the back of his head. It had been a long time since a woman had touched him with that kind of tenderness. As if he needed comforting.

It confused him. It made him angry. It soothed him to his soul.

"Damn you," he muttered, and clung to her.

"Shh," Meg said, feeling the loneliness in this man who was tormented by the past and a boy's dreams that had never stood a chance of coming true. She understood all that about him in a flash of insight that startled her as much as his sudden appearance.

And the sudden kiss.

When the embrace gentled, she pulled away from him. "Let's have some coffee, and then we'll talk."

Jordan sensed the questions she didn't ask. He was grateful for small favors. He didn't know the answers.

"Cream?" Meg asked her unexpected visitor.

"Uh, no, black is fine."

They sat at the small pine table with its colorful place mats of pink and green. The crowd of flowering plants on the windowsill seemed to watch as they took their places. The silence between them was comfortable, she found.

"I'm worried about Hope," he said finally.

"Yes," she agreed. She, too, had noticed the reserve

drawing tighter around her friend. Only with Gabe did Hope open up completely, or as much as she could.

"Do you think she's in love with the Kincaid grandson?" he asked bluntly.

"Yes."

He frowned fiercely. "Damn."

Meg smiled in sympathy, understanding much in the one word. "Men want things to be simple. You, for instance, want revenge on the Kincaids. Simple. Except it isn't. The present Kincaids aren't the source of your troubles. Neither was Jeremiah. Your uncle lost the ranch, Mr. Baxter, not Jeremiah. He was simply the vulture that settled in and fed off the Baxter troubles."

Jordan lifted his coffee cup, gesturing toward her as he did. "Don't spare my feelings," he said with more than a smidgen of sarcastic humor in the words. "Just tell me what you truly think. And call me Jordan. I think we know each other well enough for that."

She met his gaze levelly. He was a handsome man, forty-seven to her thirty-six. His eyes were gray but without the blue tints that softened his daughter's eyes to smoky shades. His body was lean, hard and muscular. She liked the fact that his wealth hadn't made him complacent and indulgent toward himself.

His concern for Hope indicated there was a softer side to his nature. His gentleness with Gabe confirmed it.

"Jordan," she said, repeating the name, acknowledging the attraction between them. She met his gaze candidly. There was interest in those depths. She felt the awakening inside her. It had been a long time since she'd wanted a man, either in her bed or otherwise.

Otherwise? As in a relationship?

A sense of wonder and alarm spread through her. "What is going on?" she asked. When he raised his eyebrows, she added, "Between us."

"I don't know," he admitted. "I'm not sure I even like it. However, I think you're the key to my daughter right now. She's closed me out."

He paused, and Meg sensed the sadness in him.

"She closed me out a long time ago," he amended. "But maybe I closed her out first. There were so many business decisions to make…"

He let the thought trail off into silence. Meg sipped the coffee and let him think on the past.

"She was a wonderful child," he continued after a while. "Sunny-natured, a smile for everyone."

"But especially for her daddy?" Meg coaxed.

He nodded. "No one had ever loved me like that—without guile or question or doubt. She was the one thing in my life that came with no strings." A frown nicked two deep creases between his eyes. He looked pensive. "Sometimes I wonder what happened to that child."

"She's still there," Meg advised. "But she's learned to be wary. Just as you did when you were young and idealistic and thought the world was there to do your bidding."

She mused on Gabe and his confidence that he could command life to his liking. That brought her back to her main worry. She stewed on it for several minutes.

"Why the heavy sigh?" Jordan finally asked, his voice once more soft, his gaze thoughtful.

"Children," she said. "And what's best for them."

"You think Collin Kincaid is best for Hope?"

She saw the worry in his eyes, which weren't so steely, after all. "Maybe. Only they can tell for sure. And only if you step out of the way."

His tone hardened. "You don't expect much from a man—just revise his whole way of thinking in the blink of an eye. I'm supposed to drop everything and embrace the Kincaid grandson because he has an itch for my daughter?"

"It's hard to know what's best in my own life," she admitted. "I really don't want to be advising others on theirs. However, you did ask my opinion."

She grinned with a certain amount of irony. After a moment he grinned back. Then, unexpectedly, they laughed.

It was the oddest thing…

Jordan entered his daughter's office without knocking on Monday morning. The secretary had said Hope was in.

He paused after closing the door. Hope looked up. Her smile was perfunctory, her gaze wary. The smoky blue-gray of her eyes shielded her thoughts.

"You remind me of your mother," he said. "I always thought she was one of the most beautiful women I ever met."

"Was that why you married her?"

The cynical undertone in the question was unexpected. Jordan considered the past before answering. "She was quiet and refined. She had the connections I needed in the top level of New York society."

"So you married her for money. Actually, to make money from her friends and family acquaintances."

"No." He thought he shouldn't have started down this path and wondered why he felt nostalgic today. "She was a safe harbor in a turbulent world. I don't know how I felt when we married, but when she died…"

The words were harder to say than he thought they would be. Hope watched him without a change in expression.

"When she died, I realized how much she'd come to mean to me. The loneliness was the worst thing I'd ever endured, more than having to leave the ranch when my uncle sold it. Sometimes it seemed you were the only thing that kept me sane during those first years after she was gone."

He watched as she placed papers in a folder and closed it, then put the folder in a drawer. Her desk, like her office, was neat. Everything about her was orderly. Too much so. Regret for things he couldn't name hit him.

Hope studied her father curiously. He seemed in an odd mood. She didn't want to discuss the past. "Was there something you needed to see me about?"

He hesitated, then said, "Kurt says the change of venue was denied."

"That's correct. I really didn't think we had much of a chance of success. However, if we lose in this round, we can go to Denver for the appeal. The Kincaids will probably file a countersuit."

A frown that once would have upset her and sent her scurrying for ways to please him creased his forehead. She regarded him without emotion, safe behind the professional distance she'd learned in law school.

"If you're already thinking of losing, the case is as good as lost," he told her, anger in his tone. "Kurt says the odds are on our side, that we can present a good argument for fraud."

Hope nodded. "That's true, but my job as your attorney is to keep all the possibilities in mind. Nothing is a sure thing."

"But death and taxes."

She observed his disgruntled expression as he added the ending of the cliché. Her father was not a patient man.

"Even those can often be delayed indefinitely." She smiled slightly. "With the help of a good doctor and a good attorney."

Her father studied her for a long, uncomfortable

minute. "I wonder if Kurt should take over. You may be too personally involved."

The suggestion surprised and stung her to the quick. She would never compromise her work. "It's your right to have council you're confident in. If you're dissatisfied, then of course you must do as you think best."

"How serious is it between you and Kincaid?"

She stiffened at what she felt was a direct attack on her integrity. "There is nothing between Collin... any of the Kincaids...and me."

Her father looked as if he didn't believe her. "I had a talk with Meg on Friday night. She thinks there could be."

Hope willed away the anger, and the rush of blood to her face, while questions hammered at her. Meg? Her father? They had talked about her and Collin?

"Does she?" she said, her tone cool and unemotional. "I have no control over what others may think."

"I only want your happiness," he said suddenly. "It doesn't lie with the Kincaids. I understand the grandson was over at your place the other night."

"I don't have to ask who reported that bit of news. The office weasel, Kurt. Correct?"

"You've changed," her father said, totally ignoring her conclusion.

She realized he'd often done that to her—ignored what he didn't want to acknowledge. It made her feel less a person than a commodity to him. The terrible achy sadness she'd experienced of late attacked her.

"You're no longer the reliable person I depended on," he continued. "Has Collin Kincaid affected you this much?"

She wasn't up to discussing Collin after the miserable weekend she'd spent. Neither did she want to bare her soul to her father. "I'm an adult. I'm responsible for my actions and well-being. I don't need anyone—"

"Stay out of the clutches of young Kincaid," her father advised harshly. "He's not to be trusted."

Quelling the onrush of resentment, she met her father's eyes calmly. "He says the same of you. He says the tapes of him and his grandfather were doctored. It would be bad enough if the court found you'd put a wiretap on someone. To also find you'd doctored the tapes to suit your purpose would put your entire case in a very questionable light."

Expecting a quick denial, Hope was troubled when Jordan shifted uncomfortably and didn't meet her eyes.

"Did you doctor the tapes?" she asked bluntly.

"No," he said quickly.

Too quickly? Confusion scattered her thoughts. She'd never doubted her father...until lately. Now her life was one big question mark. She trusted no one, not even herself.

"It's a fine day when my daughter questions my word over that of a Kincaid," he said with a snort.

"I'm your attorney," she corrected sharply. "If I'm to represent you effectively, then I have to have a good idea of what I'll be facing in court. Illegal wire-tapping isn't something I can justify to the judge."

He nodded. "It won't come to that. The trustees will back off. The Baxter place will be ours."

"Yours," she corrected. "I want no part of it."

He looked stunned at this announcement. "You're my heir," he reminded her.

"Judging by Emma's experience, the Baxter legacy hasn't been much of an asset." She couldn't believe she'd said that to her father. From his expression, he found it hard to digest, too.

He stood and glared at her. "She sold her heritage when she married one of the Kincaid bastards."

"He was the only person who believed in her innocence. She loves him." Hope defended Emma's choice.

"If you chose the Kincaid grandson over your family, I'll write you out of my will. I'll disown you—"

She stood, too. "I don't need either the Baxter or the Kincaid name to earn my place in the world."

Trembling, she held her ground and returned his disbelieving glare with enforced calm. A tempest of emotion stormed through his eyes—anger, of course, and betrayal, plus others too rapid to read. For an eternity between one breath and another, they stared at each other.

When he strode out, she pressed her palms on the

desk and breathed slowly and deeply. Her world—the one that she'd always thought was safe—was splitting into pieces, and she didn't know how to put them together again. She turned toward the window with the thought of escaping or running away, something she'd never considered in her life.

The blue of the sky reminded her of blue eyes that had met her gaze levelly.

I'll wait, Collin had said.

She had thought she could never accept that promise. Now she wasn't sure….

"It's a simple question," Jordan said. "Did you doctor the tape you gave me of Kincaid and his grandson?"

Kurt Peters smiled. Jordan realized how bland that white-toothed smile was, outlined by twin rows of perfectly aligned teeth. It irritated him.

"Let me rephrase the question. Did you make any changes whatsoever to the original conversation?"

The smile didn't falter. "I edited them somewhat. For clarity," the younger man admitted.

Jordan had a sick feeling in the pit of his stomach. "'Them,'" he repeated. "Plural. You recorded more than one conversation and put them together to make one."

The smile disappeared. Kurt's expression became very earnest, sort of perplexed, as if he couldn't figure out what he was being accused of, if anything.

"The context was the same," he said. "I would never alter that." The smile reappeared. "There was no need to. Collin Kincaid laid out his plans pretty clearly, I thought. Should I destroy the tape, sir? If it's making you uncomfortable… Maybe it's best if Hope doesn't hear it. If she's involved with Kincaid…"

Jordan studied the corporate attorney. Kurt's eyes met his candidly. No guile there. Jordan sighed. "No, no, she's not involved. Destroy the tape, or tapes, as the case may be. There's nothing we can use in them."

"Yes, sir," Kurt said. "Consider it done."

"Good. Shall we meet for lunch? Tell Hope I'd like her to join us. I want to go over the case."

"Right."

Satisfied, Jordan returned to his office. He liked to use an element of surprise when he confronted people. Kurt hadn't blinked an eye at his accusation of altering the taped telephone conversations. The sharp young attorney had been puzzled, but he'd been straightforward about "editing" the tape.

For a second Jordan wondered where Kurt had gotten the idea of wiretapping in the first place. Another thought occurred to him: what other lines had the man tapped in on?

He shook his head and picked up the telephone when it rang. He was getting more and more paranoid about trusting people as the lawsuit dragged on. He even questioned his own motives these days.

That was Meg's fault. Women made a man soft, distracted him from his quest....

"Calm down. There's nothing that can be traced to you. What's the motive?" Lexine snapped impatiently to Audra.

She glared at the girl from behind the Plexiglas partition. The warden wouldn't let her use the private reception room anymore. That privilege was for "model" prisoners.

Lexine sighed. Okay, so she'd lost her temper and thrown a bowl of stew at another prisoner, so what? She was under a lot of stress these days what with propping up Audra all the time and trying to figure out what to do since Emma—that ungrateful brat!—had gotten off the hook.

"The Indian has already been tried and convicted by the whole town," she continued.

"He's a doctor," Audra countered. "Some of the other physicians and nurses are speaking out for him. His patients are, too."

"He's already admitted to being the father of the baby as well as being on the scene to deliver it."

"He had to. I mean, DNA tests and everything."

Lexine grinned at her daughter. "Which will convict him. Don't you see, my dearest daughter? You're in the clear. It's all working out perfectly." She gave the younger woman a tender, sympathetic look. "Besides, it isn't as if you meant to kill her. It was an accident. Why should you suffer when it was the stupid girl's own fault? She shouldn't have been there in the first place."

Audra nodded. "I wish that old scarecrow, the prospector, hadn't seen me, though. He makes me nervous."

"No one will believe anything Homer Gilmore says, not after he identified Emma and was wrong, so that's no problem. You're free to start searching for the sapphire mine again."

The girl brightened at Lexine's reassuring words.

At least *this* daughter was easy to control. That Emma—ungrateful brat—hadn't wanted to help at all. She hadn't believed Lexine's explanation of the past and how the Kincaids had set her up. Too bad the girl got off the murder rap. It would have solved several problems for her and Audra. Those damn Kincaids had interfered again.

"I have some new maps," she said, unrolling the topography maps the government so conveniently provided.

She pointed out likely search areas on the old Baxter homestead. With the arrest of Gavin Nighthawk, the pressure was off Audra. She could get started on their quest once more without interference from the law.

"Here's where the original mine was," Lexine said, pointing to the area. "Here's where the new vein was located."

Anger washed over her at the memory of Homer,

who'd prospected the mountains for years, finding the sapphires that should have been hers. The gemstones, valuable for lasers used in medical research, were the reason she'd come back to Whitehorn and married that wimp, Dugan Kincaid, and put up with his lecherous old daddy, Jeremiah.

People kept getting in her way. She should have gotten rid of Homer when she had him locked in the cave used as a jail at the old mining camp years ago. She grimaced. There was no profit in dwelling on the past. She had other fish to fry, as the saying went.

"Here's where I found some loose stones in the creek. The triangle between these three places is the logical place to look. There's a logging road you can use for access. Your boyfriend, Micky What's-his-name, he'll let you use his truck, right? And he'll keep his mouth shut?"

"Oh, yes," Audra said airily. "Micky will do whatever I tell him, no questions asked."

Mother and daughter grinned at each other.

Audra felt much better by the time she left the prison and returned to the trailer. Micky was there, watching a game show on television. A dirty plate was on the beat-up coffee table, a beer bottle beside it.

She hated the…the *squalor* of her present life. Desperation seized her. It was her mother's fault— her adoptive mother's. The stupid Felicia Westwood had lost their money by trusting that crooked attorney, then had expected Audra to go to work to support the two of them. Audra despised her.

But that was the past.

The future gleamed brightly ahead. With those sapphires, she would be free of past mistakes. She'd make a new start, find a husband who was worthy of her. She studied Micky, who sprawled on the sagging sofa, and laughed at the irony of her being with someone like him.

But he had his uses.

"You seem to be in a good mood," he remarked. "What's so funny?"

"You. Me. Us. Life," she proclaimed dramatically. "How much money do you have? I feel like going out. Let's celebrate—dinner and dancing in the big town of Whitehorn in the glorious state of Montana. What do you say?"

His smile was instant. "Sure."

She turned away so he wouldn't see the contempt she couldn't disguise. He was so easy to manipulate. Too easy, really. No challenge at all.

Ten

"Mmm, fry bread," Meg said, gesturing toward a booth. "I love it. I'll have that for lunch."

Hope laughed. It was the first Monday in September. Labor Day. Meg had talked her into coming to the festivities at the Laughing Horse Reservation for the day. To her total surprise, her father had decided to join them.

"That's setting a good example for Gabe," he said with a mock-scolding glance at Meg.

Hope pushed Gabe in his shaded stroller and studied her friend and her father surreptitiously as they drifted from booth to booth. Something odd there. It was almost as if they were friends.

Or lovers.

She shied from the thought as pain clutched at her chest. Her imagination was running wild.

"Hop," Gabe said, demanding her attention. He pointed to the rabbit cages.

The three adults veered toward the livestock area. Hope viewed more types of rabbits than she had ever before known existed. At one pen, children were allowed inside to pet the furry little creatures.

"Jor," Gabe said, and held up his arms.

Dumbfounded, Hope watched as her father lifted the boy and went into the pen. He set Gabe on his feet and lifted a rabbit so the child could pet it. Speaking softly, her father told Gabe where to rub and how to touch the rabbit. He explained how rabbits hopped on their strong back legs and how fast they could run.

Gabe listened solemnly and was gentle. Jordan reminded him from time to time to be careful. The two moved on down the pen, petting and discussing various rabbits.

Hope turned a perplexed gaze on her friend. "Gabe seems to know my father."

To her further surprise, Meg blushed. "Jordan has been over to the house," she said.

"To your house?" Hope blurted. "When?"

"Uh, actually nearly every night for the past week. And a couple of times the week before," Meg added truthfully.

Hope was speechless.

Meg smiled ruefully. "I, uh, stuck my nose in

without being invited. Remember that Tuesday—it was nearly three weeks ago—when you kept Gabe because I had a wedding reception to decorate?"

As Meg recounted her impulsive decision to put in her two cents' worth to Jordan, Hope listened, half in shock, half in disbelief.

"It's a wonder my father didn't throw you out."

Meg laughed softly. "I walked out before he had the chance." She gave Hope an embarrassed glance. "I hope you'll forgive me for interfering. I had absolutely no right to do what I did."

"No. No, that's okay," Hope assured her, not sure what she thought.

"Shortly after that, the following Friday, in fact, your father stopped by the cottage. I thought he'd come to tell me to stay out of his business, but he asked me about you. He finished bathing Gabe and said he had raised you."

"My father?" Hope said as if she thought aliens had taken over his body and deceived Meg.

Meg laughed, understanding in her eyes. "Yes."

Hope studied Jordan as he knelt beside Gabe, talking softly to the inquisitive child, showing him how soft the bunny's fur was. She suddenly recalled a time when she'd been sick with the flu. Her father had made a bed for her under his desk, hidden from the sight of two businessmen who were in a meeting with him. Her presence had been their secret, and she had stayed quiet as a mouse, soothed just to be near him.

"I once thought he was wonderful," she murmured.

"He's good with children," Meg said. "I think it's easier for him to trust children and therefore be at ease with them. He learned when he was hardly more than a boy not to trust the adults in his life."

Hope nodded, her thoughts in a whirl. For the rest of the morning, she observed the other two adults. There was more than friendship between them. They were attracted to each other. It was obvious in the frequent meeting of their eyes, the casual touches, the tension between them as they shared Gabe's care.

She swallowed as her throat filled with a painful lump. Again she felt the outsider, the one who watched from the sidelines while others engaged in life.

Turning from the Norman Rockwell scene of Meg and Jordan helping Gabe eat his first fry bread with honey without getting too messy, Hope encountered a hard stare from summer-blue eyes.

Collin Kincaid watched her with a relentless gaze filled with passionate intensity. Perspiration broke out all over her, and her step faltered. Meg and her father, who was pushing Gabe in the stroller, strode on ahead of her.

Collin inclined his head slightly in greeting. He didn't smile. She forced a smile on her face, nodded back and walked hurriedly on, her heart beating very fast.

She hadn't seen him since last Wednesday, the

day of the meeting in her father's conference room, and that night, when he had shown up at her condo.

Come live with me.

What had he meant by that? Marriage? A live-in arrangement until their passion played itself out?

Her father would have a heart attack if she did, then he'd disown her just as he'd threatened. She, too, had a heritage. She couldn't toss it away because of passion and intense blue eyes.

Collin kept an eye on Hope as the day wore down into late afternoon. Her smile was as fake as a three-dollar bill. He knew. He'd seen the real Hope, and she was nothing like this quiet woman who observed the crowd at the fair from the fringes, as if she were a researcher sent to observe others at play.

She, her father and the wedding planner made an odd trio. The little boy seemed at ease with all the adults. Collin watched Jordan and Meg. If they weren't lovers, they were headed that way. That much was obvious.

Anger coursed through him. Jordan Baxter was the only obstacle between him and Hope. The man didn't deserve happiness when he denied it to his daughter.

Collin heaved a heavy sigh. Who was he to think she could only be happy with him? Hope was an adult. She had to make her own choices. Actually, she had. Only she hadn't chosen *him*.

When he saw the other attorney who worked with her on the case against the Kincaids arrive and rush over to them, he had to restrain an urge to jerk Hope out of their midst and keep her with him the rest of the day.

Or forever. Whichever came first.

As evening spread lavender fingers across the sky, the dancing started under the covered pavilion. The tribe liked to display its ceremonial dancing and explain it to the Anglos, then invite the outsiders to join in. Later the dancing would be taken over by the younger members of the Cheyenne, who would play tapes of rock 'n' roll music and do the latest gyrations to it.

He stood in back of the crowd and watched Hope as her little group watched from the sidelines. Kurt Peters tried to get Hope to dance. She refused. When the man gave up and turned to talk to her father, Hope moved a few feet away. She looked around as if searching for the nearest exit.

An impulse stirred Collin into action. He might regret it. Hell, he might end up in a fight. But Hope was worth the effort, and he couldn't stand another minute of her lawyer cohort fawning over her.

He strode over. "Evening," he said. He took her hand. "Dance?"

"No, thank you." She used her prissy back-East voice.

He grinned, the devil on his shoulder spurring him

on to recklessness. "Perhaps I'd better rephrase that. Are you coming peacefully, or do I have to drag you?"

Her eyes flew open at the threat.

"Yeah, I'm that desperate," he told her.

Her chin went up in the air. He tugged on her hand and she stepped forward. Relief speared through him. She wasn't going to fight him over the dance.

"Smart thinking," he murmured as they took their place, face-to-face, in the line of dancers.

She glared at him, her movements stiff and wooden as she moved to the tempo of the drums.

He felt the beat vibrate right down to his core as he feasted his eyes on the woman he hadn't seen in nearly a week.

"I've missed you," he said honestly.

"Don't."

"Don't miss you or don't say it?"

"Don't be impossible."

Her eyes almost pleaded. Guilt gnawed at him, along with the hunger and the need that was more than hunger. "Don't make it so hard for us."

She glanced from side to side as if to see if anyone had heard him. Her lips were pressed tightly closed. He remembered how soft they were, how responsive.

He took her hand and moved closer. "Come away with me."

She jerked free, panic in her eyes.

"To Elk Springs," he continued softly, soothing her as if she were the filly he was training for his sister. "There are some beautiful spots in the Bitterroot Mountains, too. There's one on the ranch next to the river where we could picnic…and then make love under the stars."

Her mouth dropped open in a silent gasp before she snapped it closed. She gave him a repressive glare.

He grinned and dared her with his eyes. When she missed a step, he caught both her hands and held them as they moved in time to the powerful beat of the drums, faster and faster, moving in a circle of writhing humanity joined in the elemental force of music and movement.

When the music stopped, he held on to her hands. "I've *really* missed you."

"Huh. Kincaids miss having every woman they meet falling at their feet."

He frowned at her cynical tone, then grinned. "It could get mighty crowded considering the number of us. I don't believe Gina would allow many women to pile up around Trent's feet. Leanne would string up any female who came on to Cade and leave her carcass for the buzzards."

Someone put on a tape of popular tunes. The first one was a slow love song. Without giving Hope a chance to protest, Collin took her in his arms.

The heat from his lean masculine body invaded her, melting some part that was icy and rigid. Her muscles loosened, and she moved with greater ease than she had on the first dance.

"That's better," he said, resting his chin against her temple.

She spotted Kurt Peters watching them from the edge of the crowd, his eyes flat and cold. Meg and her father sat on a bench under a scrawny cottonwood while Gabe ate a drippy ice-cream cone. While she watched, Jordan touched Meg's hand, squeezed it, then bent to wipe a long slurp of chocolate ice cream from Gabe's mouth.

"Your father has found a lady friend," Collin remarked.

She looked up and found sympathy in his eyes, which were warm and tender. Caring.

But men were always warm and tender and caring when they got their own way. Her father was a prime example with his unpredictable temper that lashed out without warning, particularly since his return to Whitehorn.

"I hope he doesn't hurt her…"

She wished she hadn't voiced the worry. She didn't want her friend to be disappointed. Neither did she want to lose Meg because of her father's interest, which was probably temporary at best. He'd never maintained a male-female relationship for long. His work came first.

And his need for revenge.

She forced the thought away, feeling it was a betrayal on her part. Her father sought justice, not revenge.

"What?" Collin asked as if sensing her turmoil.
"Nothing."

He was silent after that. When the song ended, he
led her out of the dancers and away from where her
party waited for her. "Emma is here. She was asking
about you this morning. She said she left word at
your office yesterday for you to call. She thought
you two might have lunch this weekend if you had
a free moment."

"Yes, she did. I was busy."

"Don't follow in your father's footsteps and cut
out those who want to be friends with you," he
advised, acting the wise older one. "Including me.
Especially me."

She stiffened. "If you truly want to be my friend,
then leave me alone."

Now he was the one who tensed. "Not a chance,"
he said with a brief shake of his handsome head.

She turned away from the sheer appeal of him.
"The situation is too complicated between us,
between our families," she corrected. "There will
never be anything between us."

"Coward," he said softly, and walked away.

She spun around, but he was already gone,
mingling in the crowd, a tough man who walked
with the assurance of one who knew his place in the
world and was secure in it.

She wished she were half as certain of her own.
She returned to Meg and her father. Lifting Gabe in

her arms, she volunteered to take him home and put him to bed, thus letting the couple have some time on their own.

"Oh, no, I wouldn't saddle my worst enemy with Gabe tonight. He'll be cranky and probably impossible after such a busy day," Meg protested.

Jordan smiled at Meg. "Let's take advantage. I feel like dancing for the first time in years."

In the end Hope, succeeding in wresting Gabe from his guilt-ridden mom, drove home in Meg's car, which had a car seat. Kurt had been gracious when she'd said good-night, but she had sensed his anger.

She couldn't believe he thought he had a chance with her. Her father's yes-man, who somehow spied on her and reported her moves to her elder? She trusted him about as far as she could throw him. Which would likely be from her office window.

With a sardonic smile, she bundled Gabe into the house, gave him a quick bath and had him tucked into bed by nine. He gave her a damp kiss and was asleep before his head hit the pillow.

She watched him for a minute, her heart tight and achy. Men had careers and families. Why was it so hard for a woman to do the same?

Jordan laid his hand flat in the middle of Meg's tummy. Her skin was soft, smooth and still slightly damp from their lovemaking. "I don't want to talk about it."

He had dropped her at her cottage before eleven, said good-night and gone home. His daughter's car had been in the drive. At midnight, he'd returned.

A light had been on, and Hope's car was gone.

Meg had greeted him in her nightgown and robe. She hadn't been surprised to see him. "I waited," she said simply when he stepped inside and shut the door.

When he took her in his arms, the world had seemed right. For that instant.

"Did you see his eyes when they danced?" Meg went on as if he hadn't spoken.

"No."

"He's in love with her, Jordan. You're going to have to accept that. Hope loves him, too."

"To hell with that." Fury burned in him at the betrayal of his own flesh and blood.

Meg sighed and snuggled close. She planted kisses on his chest and rubbed his back as if he were a child. She confused him with her quick barbs and her tender ways.

"Look into your heart," she advised. "Are you being fair to Hope? She could have a future with Collin."

"What makes you think his intentions are honorable? He's using her to gain insights into how we're going to present our case."

"Do you really think so?"

"I know so. Kurt taped a conversation of him talking to his grandfather, telling him how he had

Hope eating out of his hand." He shook his head. "I'm disappointed in Hope, falling for the Kincaid charm."

Meg was silent for a minute, her expression pensive. He supposed he'd better get up and go home. The closeness induced by their lovemaking was gone.

"What are your intentions toward me and my son?" she asked before he could move.

"I—" He tried to think, but the question had thrown him for a loop. "I haven't thought that far ahead," he said slowly, watching her green eyes as he spoke.

She sighed. "I can't allow you a place in my life if it's going to be a here-today-gone-tomorrow relationship. My son is young enough to form a lasting attachment. It would hurt him too much. Neither will I be a convenience for you."

He flung himself out of bed. "Women always have to complicate things," he muttered, throwing his clothes on as fast as he could.

She rose and pulled on a robe. "No. I merely want to be up front with you," she corrected, a smile tinged with sadness playing over her expressive lips. "It isn't all going to be your way. I have needs, too. So does my son. If you want to be in our lives, you have to earn the right, then you have to respect it."

She spoke firmly, but her eyes were lambent. He felt their caress as if she stroked his heart. There was no anger in her, only an honesty that was open and refreshing. He couldn't just walk away.

He dropped his shirt and peeled off his jeans. "It'll be on your terms," he heard himself say.

She smiled and held out her arms. Grateful, he stepped into the embrace and felt her heat warm him all the way through. It had been a long time since he'd felt so…so…

Welcome.

Yeah, that was the word.

"I want you and the boy to move in with me. My house is big enough for all of us."

"That can only be through marriage," she murmured, kissing his throat.

His body hardened with need. "Okay."

She pressed her hands to each side of his face. "Let's think this through carefully. I don't want to make any mistakes. And we have Hope to consider."

Confused, half angry again, he lifted her in his arms. "I'm considered a good catch by some women."

"Huh," she snorted. "You're arrogant and obsessed with a piece of land not much good for anything. But there's goodness in you, too. I think you can be saved in spite of yourself."

He didn't understand that at all, but he would think about it later. Much later. He carried the frustrating, utterly fascinating woman to bed and using all his powers of persuasion tried to convince her marriage was the best thing for them. Dumbfounded, he realized he meant it.

* * *

Hope pushed the papers into her briefcase and headed for her car. It was nearly 9:00 p.m., and she was dead-tired. After a restless night spent dreaming of a duel between Collin and her father—she didn't need a psychologist to figure that one out—she'd had another confrontation with Jordan over Kurt's involvement in the case.

Her presentation was clear and logical. Even her father had conceded that. She didn't need a man to do the opening statement for her. Kate Randall Walker was known to be scrupulously fair as a judge. They would be lucky to get her.

Right now, the court was tied up with the Nighthawk case. It didn't look good for the young doctor. He needed a break, some bit of evidence that would definitely clear him. Not even Perry Mason could make a case out of thin air for Nighthawk.

Another thing that bothered Hope was her father's suggestion that Collin had danced with her yesterday at the tribal festivities only to embarrass the Baxters. She had turned the tables when she'd asked him why he had stayed with her and Meg all day.

He had actually blushed. So there had been something to her intuition about them.

"Don't hurt Meg," she'd advised him coolly. "She doesn't need a short-term romance."

"I'm not offering one," he'd said just as icily. "Our relationship is none of—"

He'd stopped before finishing the sentence. Even he could see the double standard in declaring his relationship off limits while hers was fair game.

"'Relationship'?" she'd asked, pouncing on the word as she'd been trained by some of the finest legal minds in the world. "Has it gone that far?"

They had reached an impasse. She had looked him straight in the eye, then walked out of his office.

Sighing tiredly, she realized she hadn't had anything since a light lunch. She hadn't anything she could prepare quickly at the condo. Seeing a parking space, she pulled into it and walked across the street to the Hip Hop. They made excellent soup.

At thirty minutes before closing, the odd little diner had few customers. Hope took a seat at the counter, ordered the soup special of the day with cornbread, then stared at the wall when the waitress left.

Only it wasn't the wall. It was a mirror. Reflected in it was a man she would recognize on the dark side of the moon. Collin. He was with a woman.

The pain was so swift, so violent, it was as if she'd been shot in the abdomen. She looked away, staring at anything but the man and the woman seated at an intimate table for two in the far corner.

She couldn't stay. She couldn't leave. She sat there, grounded to the spot by forces too powerful for her to overcome at that moment.

"Here you go, ma'am," the waitress said, placing

her food in front of her. After asking if Hope needed anything more, she went back to cleaning behind the counter.

Hope picked up the spoon. An icy rage settled around her heart. She would eat the soup if it choked her. Never would she break and run in front of an enemy. Especially a Kincaid. She forced one spoonful down. Another. Then another.

She was almost finished when she heard footsteps behind her. They stopped at the cash register, which was at the counter three stools from her.

"Hello, Hope," Collin said in a quiet voice.

She looked at him then. He was dressed in black slacks and a white shirt. The sleeves were casually rolled back, disclosing corded muscles. She looked at his hands, which had several little scars from various encounters in his ranch work—a stubborn cow and a barbed-wire fence, a horse who'd bit him when he was a kid, a fish hook—

Looking up, she met his eyes. "Good evening." She sounded haughty and disapproving. Unable to hold his gaze, she glanced away, then looked quickly down at her bowl.

The woman, young and pretty, stood by the door, waiting while the waitress accepted payment from Collin, then counted out his change. Collin took the money, but didn't leave.

"Are you okay?" he asked.

"Of course." But she wouldn't have been surprised

to find her lifeblood pooling at her feet, she felt so wounded, so betrayed, so incredibly hurt.

"Did you have a good time at the reservation?"

"It was fine."

She heard him release a deep breath, but she didn't look at him. Neither could she think of anything to say.

"I'll be at Whitehorn for a couple of days, then I'll have to spend the rest of the week in Elk Springs. I'll come back next Saturday."

Please go away. "Yes, well, have a nice trip," she said, swallowing against the tears suddenly blocking her throat. Why wouldn't he leave?

Finally she heard him walk off. She managed to breathe once more. She glanced at her watch, then laid a ten on the counter. "Here's my money. Keep the change," she called to the young waitress who was cleaning off Collin's table.

"Thanks. Have a nice evening," the waitress called, flashing Hope a smile.

She hurried out into the night, glad for the darkness, glad for the chilly wind that cooled her hot face and stanched the bleeding of her heart. She made it home and to her condo without seeing another person.

Inside, she showered and changed into a nightgown, then took two aspirin and drank a glass of milk. Her stomach formed a knot around the food and hurt. She sat in the darkness and argued with her foolish, foolish heart.

He was with another woman.

Maybe it was his sister or another relative.

He doesn't care.

He asked about your health. He thought you looked ill.

It didn't mean anything.

Maybe it did.

Go away. Leave me alone. I can't bear it.

You could have had him. Him and his love. You threw it away.

I didn't. It was never there. He was using me, just as my father said.

And in the end it wasn't Collin and thoughts of him with another woman that broke through her reserve. It was the message on her answering machine from Meg. The thought of little Gabe, of having sweet babies with a loving man—that was what dealt the final blow to her control.

Harsh, gasping sounds tore from her body, but her eyes stayed dry as dust. She pressed a hand to her heart and by trying with all her might, forced the pain at bay. Dawn streaked the sky before she fell asleep.

Eleven

Hope approved a revision in wording to the company's policy and procedures manual and laid the document in her Out basket for Selma to handle. She pinched the bridge of her nose where a headache pounded.

Glancing at her watch, she saw she'd worked through dinner again. She'd been doing that often of late. She'd cleared every memo and letter and e-mail. Her desk was as pristine as new-fallen snow.

Swiveling the desk chair, she studied the night sky. No stars gleamed through the clouds that had gathered all day. In midafternoon, a hailstorm had blown through, leaving hard white balls of ice on the streets and lawns of the town, pinging against windows and roofs with a harsh wintry sound, the herald of the season to come.

It was only September.

Ranchers were busy getting the last hay harvest baled. Cattle were being moved down from the high ranges to home pastures. The brood cows would be separated from their babies and the calves sold to feed lots.

Recalling the soft brown eyes of the yearlings at the Kincaid ranch, she experienced a moment's sadness, then hardened her heart. It was the way of things.

A knock brought her around to face the door. "Come in."

Kurt entered her office. "Hi," he said. His smile was tentative, almost shy. "Thought I saw you burning the midnight oil. Finished?"

"Yep, all done." She consciously injected a note of friendliness in her tone. She'd been pretty distant to everyone this week, ever since the day after Labor Day when she'd seen Collin with the Native American woman.

"You, uh, interested in dinner?"

"Yes," she said, determined to get over the depression that had haunted her since that night.

Kurt looked so surprised, she had to smile. "How about the Black Boot? It's supposed to have great steaks."

The Black Boot was a honky-tonk out on the highway popular with the cowboys on weekends.

"It's Friday. The place will be crowded," she reminded him. Besides, she didn't want to be around cowboys and ranchers. "How about the Hip Hop?"

"Sure."

His tone was casual, but his smile was so grateful, she felt guilty at being so cold to him lately. He was really a nice guy and a smart attorney. Her father was probably right. She would go far before finding someone else so suited to her in interests and loyalties.

"I'll meet you there in…five minutes?"

"Right on." He gave her a two-fingered salute and disappeared, closing the door quietly behind him.

Hope sighed, then realized that she had. No being in the doldrums, she admonished as she locked up. Adopting a cheerful pose, she headed out to her car and drove the short distance to the local restaurant. Kurt was already there.

He stood until she was seated, then handed her a menu. She laid it aside. "I'll have vegetable soup and cornbread."

"I'll have the same."

It irritated her that he had copied her order. She quelled the feeling. Why was she being so critical? Assuming a relaxed smile, she inquired, "So, how's it going with the bank merger? Dad said you were advising on that."

Kurt waggled his hand, fingers spread. "So-so," he admitted. "The directors of the smaller bank are making some unreasonable demands."

"My father must find that annoying," she said blandly.

"Somewhat."

Their eyes met in mutual understanding of Jordan Baxter when he was thwarted. Hope smiled. A grin split Kurt's face.

He was a good-looking man with his stylishly cut brown hair and light blue eyes. He was sharp and sophisticated, with the same basic background as she had—an Ivy League education, a career in law and a position at Baxter Development Corporation. They had similar interests.

He was also ambitious and cunning, another part of her warned, refusing to embrace her father's trusted advisor.

"My secretary tells me you've bought a place in the complex where I live," she mentioned, turning the conversation from corporate interests.

"Yes, directly across the lake from your place. I decided it was time to put down roots."

They discussed the advantages of a town house over an apartment. Whitehorn was not exactly a mecca of modernity when it came to places to rent. Most apartments were in converted Victorians left from early mining days when sapphire prospectors thought they were going to be rich forever. That had quickly petered out.

The meal passed pleasantly enough, Hope decided. Kurt insisted on paying for both of them. She didn't argue, but again it annoyed her. The event wasn't a date, but a casual meal between two colleagues. For now, that was the way she wanted to keep it.

He followed behind her on the way home. Another vehicle followed behind Kurt's expensive sedan. When she'd driven off from the Hip Hop, a pickup, coming down the street, had made a U-turn and fallen in behind them.

Her heart pounded hard when she pulled into her garage. Kurt stopped in guest parking and joined her.

"Am I supposed to be doing anything else on the Kincaid case?" he asked. "Do you want me there when it goes before the judge?"

"I thought my father had assigned you to assist."

"You're the leader of the team. What do you want?"

She was touched by his concession. "To get it over and off my back," she answered with total candor. Again they smiled at each other in understanding of the elder Baxter's ways. "Would you like to come in for coffee? I have the file with me. We could go over our arguments."

"Great. I've been worried that you might get run over by a logging truck or decide to quit suddenly and I'd be left holding the bag."

While she put on coffee, she contemplated Kurt's casual remark and why he thought she might quit. Because of her difficulties with her father over Collin Kincaid, no doubt, but did everyone in the company know that? Or only her father's right-hand man?

Resentment sizzled through her like the bright red-and-gold pinwheels of her favorite fireworks. Her father confided in Kurt, evidently trusted him more than he did her.

Why should that surprise her? Jordan had always wanted a son to carry on his various business enterprises.

Kurt fed that vanity by being Johnny-on-the-spot to her father's demands. Instead of disagreeing or pointing out flaws in Jordan's thinking, he found ways to make the older man's wishes feasible.

Dislike rose in her once more. She quelled it, recalling her decision to be kinder and more open-minded where Kurt was concerned. After all, the man was simply doing his job, pleasing his employer with his skills and knowledge. It was a fault within herself that she couldn't do the same.

But more and more, she thought her father was wrong. About the Kincaids. About the company's rampant development. Of course, they were conducting environmental studies. That was good. The influx of wealthy baby boomers spurred the town's economy and added to the tax roles.

Still she worried. Was there too much growth, too soon? New schools and parks had to be planned and built. That took time. Roads and street congestion had to be considered.

She shook her head as she poured the coffee and joined Kurt in the living room. He had turned on the

CD player, which now played soft classical piano melodies in the background.

"I hope you don't mind," he said, gesturing toward the machine. "I find music soothes the soul after a busy day fighting the corporate enemies."

Hope nodded. "Did you get the permit for the final phase of the condo complex from the city? Dad was worried about that."

"Yes, it came through. No problem."

"Did you buy off the commissioners?" she asked suddenly, for no reason other than the question popped to the top of her head.

His smile was conspiratorial. "Now that would be telling."

She laughed when he did, as if they were joking, but an uneasy feeling settled in her stomach. Why did she distrust everything Kurt did for no reason while she'd trusted Collin when she had every reason not to?

Kurt closed his eyes and leaned his head back on the sofa. She was silent as the music, soft and seductive, wafted around them. It didn't reach the emptiness inside her.

When he opened his eyes as the melody died away, she saw desire in the pale blue depths. Her insides tightened nervously. "I'll get my notes," she said, putting them firmly on a business basis. "We can use the dining room table. It has more room."

She turned off the CD player and retrieved her

briefcase. They worked until midnight, then she told him it was time to quit. She escorted him to the door.

She realized his intention just before he leaned over and brushed his lips across hers, so quickly a protest would have seemed like overreaction.

"Goodnight," she said firmly, and closed the door as quickly as possible. She wiped the back of her hand over her lips, then rubbed it on her skirt.

In bed, she tried to sleep, but couldn't. She kept remembering how other lips had felt against hers. She hadn't imagined the fire between her and Collin. She'd felt none of it with Kurt.

Why?

Her heart contracted into a painful ball of undeniable truth. Because she had fallen in love with Collin Kincaid.

He had set her body on fire and her world aglow. It was unreasonable. It was foolish. But it was true. She loved him…loved him….

The words echoed with each beat of her heart. How could she have been so stupid?

She sighed unhappily. How could she have stopped it? That was the real question.

Collin laughed at the story Summer had just finished telling him about giving a shot to an infant who was determined not to take it.

His cousin, the daughter of Jeremiah Kincaid's youngest sister, was working on her residency in immunology at Whitehorn Memorial Hospital and running a clinic on the reservation in her spare time. He had only recently met her.

Summer had the dark hair and eyes of her Native American father, a man she had never known. She wore her hair pulled severely back from her face, and her eyes were mostly hidden behind glasses. She was a dedicated medical researcher who had studied herbs and alternate medicine with an aim to join the two for the benefit of her patients.

Jeremiah's other two sisters had raised her when her mom had died shortly after giving birth, she'd explained, but they had also exposed her to her Native heritage and let her spend summers at the res where she'd studied with elders who knew the old cures.

Collin had met Summer through Serena Dovesong, who was married to his half brother, Blake Remmington, Trent's twin. Blake and Serena had a son, born six years before Blake returned to Whitehorn to discover his old lover and the son he hadn't known he had.

Lucky Blake. He was now settled in his pediatrics practice with the love of his life and a great kid to come home to.

"What?" he said, realizing Summer was looking at him expectantly.

"Has any news come up about the other grandson?"

"Oh. No. Gina hasn't mentioned anything recently. I don't think." He wasn't always attentive to the dinner conversation at the ranch.

"Forgive my interest. I just find everything about our family fascinating. It's like discovering a civilization just over the mountain when you thought you were nearly the only human left. Of course I know Wayne and Clint and Jenny, but I rarely get to see them. We're all so busy."

"I know what you mean. I've been amazed at how easy it is to avoid someone in a town the size of Whitehorn."

Her smile was quick and filled with interest. "Are you the avoider or the avoidee? You don't have to answer if you don't want to," she added.

"She's avoiding me." The dark pit that had formed inside him stirred at the thought of Hope.

"Ah," Summer said, inviting discussion but not prying.

Collin shrugged. Hell, everybody on the ranch knew about his love life, why shouldn't Summer? "Hope Baxter is the attorney for her father in the lawsuit. She and I had a few meetings, trying to come to a solution, but no good came of it."

"Except you fell in love with her," Summer said softly, sympathetically. "And she with you."

"What makes you think that?" he asked cynically.

"I see it in your eyes. Love quickly withers if it isn't returned, but yours was."

"She never said she cared anything about me," he explained truthfully. "She's seeing someone else. Another attorney in her father's corporation."

"Hmm, that makes it tough, but don't give up. A person shouldn't give up on the one he or she loves."

"Are you in love?" he asked, glad to turn the tables and get off the subject of himself. His grandfather was forever prodding him to go see Hope. What he'd seen—her with another man—hadn't set well with him.

She laughed. "I have too much to do. I don't have the energy for dates by the time my day is over."

"Some stupid men are letting a good chance go by."

"Thanks for being so gallant, but I'm not in any hurry. With the work at the clinic and trying to finish my residency, I'm booked up for the next couple of years. Right now, I have other things to think about."

"Gavin Nighthawk?" Collin suggested.

Summer had asked Garrett to see if Elizabeth Gardener would take Nighthawk's case. Garrett had talked to the young doctor and believed his story. Elizabeth, at Garrett's request, had also talked to Gavin and agreed to take the case.

"Yes. The evidence against him is circumstantial, but it looks bad. A one-night stand with Christina and the fact that he delivered the baby and took it to the reservation for safekeeping, leaving Christina alone in the woods. But Christina was dead when he returned for her. Gavin would never kill anyone."

"A man will do desperate things when pushed too far."

"Gavin is innocent," she said firmly. Her gaze was open, earnest. "I've known him since we were kids from the summers I spent on the res. He's a healer, not a killer. I'd stake my life on it. But he's also proud. He would never have asked for help." She gazed off into the distance. "It's terrible not to be trusted. Some of the people saying the worst things about him are those who sang his praises when he saved their lives."

"Yeah," Collin agreed, "it hurts not to be trusted."

"Is that the problem between you and Hope?"

He smiled ruefully. "It's the classic case of the Montagues versus the Capulets. Except Juliet is not siding with Romeo in this version."

"Then she's being a very foolish woman."

"Thanks, cuz. May I quote you on that the next time I see her? If ever," he added grimly.

"Be my guest. Uh-oh, I've got to run. I've discovered a wonderful new mold that might be the next best thing to penicillin. Thanks for lunch and the conversation."

"It was a pleasure." That was true. He liked this newly discovered cousin. She was smart and dedicated and loyal to her friends.

They parted outside the Hip Hop. Collin headed for his truck, then sidetracked to the little town park down the street. It was empty now that school had started back for the year. He liked its loneliness. It matched the way he felt.

Right, feel sorry for yourself, he scoffed. That solves a lot of problems.

Propping one foot on a concrete bench, he gazed at the mountains south of town. The Beartooth peaks were dusted with new snow that had fallen yesterday. Whitehorn had gotten some hail out of the storm. Winter was in a hurry to get started this year.

He felt its chill in his heart. He shook his head, wondering how he could have been so stupid as to go and fall for a woman so obviously wrong for him. As if the thought conjured up the image, Hope appeared before his eyes.

He blinked.

She was still there. She stopped beside her car and returned his gaze, her expression as surprised as his.

Without thinking, he crossed the lawn to the sidewalk along the curb. "Hello," he said, his voice husky with passion he couldn't deny.

"Hi." She tossed her packages into the back seat of her car and slammed the door. "Well, I have to go."

The absurdity of her statement struck them both at the same time. Their eyes met and they laughed.

When they stopped, he didn't want to look away from her smoky eyes. All the hot, impatient hunger that had disturbed his dreams surged through him. He saw the answering flame ignite in her eyes.

"This is crazy," he muttered. "Let's go."

"Where?" she asked in confusion.

"Anywhere. I'll follow you home."

"No," she blurted, then in a calmer tone, "No, that wouldn't be a good idea."

"To my place then."

"The ranch?"

He frowned. "Most of the grandsons and their families are in for the weekend. Come for a drive."

Hope couldn't resist the need to be with him, to talk to him once more, just the two of them. When he took her hand, she didn't protest. Without a word she went with him to his pickup and let him lift her inside.

He quickly slid in and drove off, heading out the road toward the ranch. He passed the ranch turnoff, though, and went to the next road. Minutes flew like seconds as he navigated the old logging track. At last he stopped under the shade of an oak. Nearby was a tiny log cabin, the kind cowboys used while out on the trail.

The afternoon sun warmed the inside of the truck. Hope felt drowsy and content. For once, she didn't want to ask questions, but only to bask in the quiet surprise of being with him and not fighting. Next month in court would be time enough for that.

"The court date is set for October," she murmured, reminding him of the confrontation.

"I know. It doesn't matter."

He laid one arm on the steering wheel and twisted sideways to face her, one leg drawn up on the leather bench seat. She felt the warmth of his knee near her thigh. Her flesh immediately felt feverish there.

"We're in the middle of roundup at both the ranches," he said. "I come in and fall in bed too tired to think most nights. But then I dream."

"Of what?"

"Of this."

When he leaned over to her, she was ready. Their lips met in a burst of consuming heat. There were no words, she realized. None.

The conflagration burned through the icy poise that had been her only defense against the terrible pain of being without him and thinking of him with another woman.

She turned her face from the kiss.

"What?" he asked.

"You were with someone else." She stopped, not sure what to say, what the protocol was.

He frowned, then his brow cleared. "My cousin, Summer. Dr. Kincaid. She has a clinic on the reservation. Don't you know there can be no one else?" he demanded softly, yanking gently on her hair until she turned back to him.

His lips were rapacious on hers. She was just as hungry, just as needy, for the feel of him. She wound her arms around his shoulders. He shifted and she was across his lap, with him scooting to her side of the seat.

Collin pulled her shirt from her slacks, then his hands were on her, sliding over her smooth back, finding the strap of her bra and disposing of it in one quick twist. He heard her nearly silent moan as she moved against him, demanding more. He wanted to give her everything he was capable of.

"I want us so sated with pleasure we won't be able

to think," he told her fiercely. He slid his hands around until he could cup both her breasts. "Until we're both so dizzy we can't stand."

"Yes," she agreed.

He liked the fact that she was breathless, that she wanted him the same way he wanted her—totally, until there was nothing left but the place where they came together and passion so explosive it blew the world apart.

Shudders ran over him when he felt her fingers on his shirt, then air as she opened one button after another. He did the same to her. Together they pushed the material off each other. He gathered both shirts and tossed them on the dash. Her bra followed immediately.

"You're beautiful," he said.

"So are you."

They smiled. He felt the world slow. In town and on the road, he had raced against time and a reality that might intrude at any moment. Now there was just them.

"I've missed you," she said. "Terribly."

"You only had to call. You have my cell phone number."

"I couldn't."

He understood her pride and the loyalty that warred with the need inside her. He understood her doubts and the passion that refused to die in the face of uncertainty. He felt each and every one of those things.

Hope felt every inch of her skin ignite as he caressed her over and over. When he dipped his head and tenderly nuzzled her breasts until the nipples stood up hard and erect, she whimpered in delight and urged him closer with her hand in his hair.

She stroked his shoulders, the smooth flesh of his back and the rough, wiry hair of his chest. She found the snap on his jeans and pulled. It parted with a muted pop, muffled by the pressure of their bodies against each other.

Sliding her hand inside, she explored him thoroughly, his hot masculine desire palpable against her fingers.

"I want you," she whispered, "more than I ever thought possible, more than air…"

"More than anything I've ever known," he told her. "I'm shaking…and hurting. That's what you do to me."

When he opened her slacks, she pushed herself off him. He stripped her clothing down in one smooth motion of controlled impatience. Lifting himself, he did the same with his jeans and briefs. He quickly fitted a condom in place.

"Face me," he ordered, his hands at her waist to help.

She turned and straddled his lean, muscular hips, then instinctively rubbed against him. She was moist and ready, but he didn't allow her to settle on him. Instead he encouraged her to move however she wished while he stroked her intimately.

"Collin, I'm going to explode," she warned at one point, dropping her head back and closing her eyes tightly while she panted and sought control.

He chuckled and planted kisses along her throat and down to each breast. "Raise up."

She did. He let her settle on him, their bodies merging slowly while they watched.

"Mating," he whispered. "The miracle of birth and renewal. It's as old as time, as new as a sunrise."

Her heart trembled at his words. He was gentle and romantic and all the things she needed him to be.

"Oh, darling," she said as the climax roared closer. "Hold me. Hold me, Collin. Forever."

She knew he replied, but the words were lost in the cataclysm of sensation that pounded through her. Everything disappeared in that moment.

Then she was floating, draped against him, languid and exhausted and elated. His arms held her tightly until she came back to earth. It was a long time.

"Will you stay?" he said when she raised her head and gazed at him. "We can spend the weekend in the cabin. There's food and bedding, a pump for water."

"I can't."

She saw anger darken his eyes, but he nodded. When she started to move away, he held her. "Not yet. If this is all, then I want it to last as long as possible."

"Not long. I'm having dinner with Meg and my father tonight."

He gave her an inquiring look.

"They're involved. I worry about her, that he'll hurt her. Women haven't lasted long in his life."

"She's an adult." He traced decreasing circles over her breasts until he spiraled in on her nipples, which immediately contracted. His eyes crinkled at the corners as he smiled in satisfaction. "So are you. All grown up. All woman. All mine," he whispered as he kissed her again.

She was surprised that he was ready again so soon. Then she was surprised to discover she was, too.

"When will I see you again?" Collin asked, wary now that they were back in town.

Hope had been quiet on the return trip. He could feel her withdrawing, assuming her business persona again. He sighed and wondered if his life was to be a series of stolen moments. Lovesick. He understood the term now.

"I don't know."

"Don't close me out."

"I'm not. I don't mean to, but…"

"But?"

"I can't embarrass my father by seeing you. When the trial is over, then maybe…maybe things will be different."

He laughed briefly, scornfully. "If by 'different' you think he'll suddenly be friends with the Kincaids, think again."

She nodded, her eyes troubled. "But until then, I

can't see you. It would be a betrayal. He'd think of it that way."

Collin leaned in the window of her car where she sat in the driver's seat. "You don't want to hurt him. What about me?"

Her eyes were dark and hopeless. "I don't want to hurt you, either. The passion between us...I don't understand it, where it came from, why it's so strong, so demanding. I need you until I can't think for it."

He laid his thumb on her bottom lip and brushed back and forth. "It's more than passion. You know it. Don't you?" he demanded, needing that one confession from her.

She hesitated a long time before she nodded, but her eyes remained unhappy.

"I want to take you to Elk Springs. There's a whole new world waiting there. It'll be just the two of us, no other family members in the way. Just us and the great big Montana sky and ten thousand acres to explore."

"It may be impossible," she warned him. "I'm still a Baxter. You're still a Kincaid."

He pressed her lips closed. "I don't want to hear about the impossibilities. After the trail—one month and one week away from Monday—then I come for you. Wherever you are. In a meeting with a whole roomful of lawyers. At your father's house. Wherever you are."

She didn't answer, but turned the key in the

ignition. He saw her eyes widen in alarm. Following her line of sight, he spotted Kurt Peters, the other attorney who was working with Hope on the lawsuit. Collin knew the man would report him and Hope being together to her father.

"If there's trouble, call me," he told her. "Better yet, come to me. Promise."

He stepped aside when she nodded. She eased away from the curb and headed south out of town. He climbed into his truck and headed north, then northwest when he turned onto the highway. From town to the ranch seemed a vast distance, the miles too far to span with only his love for Hope as the building tool.

Twelve

Hope spotted Meg as soon as she entered the Hip Hop. Meg saw her, too, and motioned for her to join her and two other women at a table. Hope recognized Lily Mae Wheeler, widow—also divorcée, although Lily Mae didn't mention that often—and the main branch of the town grapevine. The other woman was Winona Cobbs, who ran a junk shop called the Stop-n-Swap. Winona was the local psychic.

Forcing a smile, Hope joined the three women. After ordering elk hash, the usual Tuesday special, she asked after her favorite person. "How's Gabe? Did that other tooth come in?"

"Yes. He's fine. Jordan is teaching him to play checkers." Meg rolled her eyes, then grinned. As if seeing the worry in Hope's eyes, Meg added, "He's really wonderful with Gabe. And to me."

Hope nodded. Maybe her father was truly in love with Meg. Maybe he would marry her and start a new life apart from Baxter Development Corporation and the lawsuit. If that happened, she could leave with a clear conscience…

Stunned at the thought, she lost track of the conversation while she tried to figure out what she meant. Was she going to leave Whitehorn or just Baxter Development? Perhaps she would open her own office. The possibilities suddenly seemed endless.

Would she, could she, go to Collin? Or were his words but empty promises, used to gain her trust as her father so contemptuously told her.

She bit her lip against a sigh of longing. Saturday seemed so long ago. Three days. Forever.

When she was with Collin, it was easy to believe everything he said and all it implied. In his arms, she dreamed impossible things. That they could marry and have beautiful, inquisitive little boys like Gabe. That her father would forget his grudge against the Kincaids. That they could be one big happy family…

"I say he's guilty as sin," Lily Mae said emphatically.

Hope, jarred out of her introspection, looked at Meg inquiringly.

"Gavin Nighthawk," Meg explained.

The scandal surrounding the trial had replaced the

feud between the Baxters and Kincaids as the main topic of conversation among the local population.

"He's innocent," Winona stated.

"I guess you got one of your vibes," Lily Mae said, looking disgruntled at being contradicted.

Winona smiled and tucked a silver strand of hair back into the coronet of braids forming a halo around her face. Turquoise earrings brought out the pale blue of her eyes. "I think he's telling the truth. It's just a feeling, but very strong. Crystal thinks so, too."

Winona was probably in her seventies, a mysterious little woman who caused as much speculation and disagreement among the townsfolk with her "visions" as the murder trial was doing. Her niece, Crystal, had caused some consternation among the local police when it was discovered she had used her psychic abilities to help Sloan Ravencrest, one of the investigating officers in the case. It was Crystal whose vision, insight, or whatever one might call it, had helped Sloan find Christina's body.

"Winona was right about the baby being alive and well," Meg reminded Lily Mae.

"The evidence points conclusively to Dr. Nighthawk," Lily Mae insisted. "Baby Alyssa was proven by DNA testing to be Gavin's child. She mysteriously appeared at her aunt Rachel's house with a note to take care of her until the father could come for her. That note was written by Gavin. He's confessed to everything but the murder, including being in the woods with her and delivering the baby."

"But," Hope said, "there's one other person not accounted for."

The three women looked at her.

"The twin. Emma's twin."

"Huh," Lily Mae snorted. "If there is such a person."

"There is," Winona said.

Hope nodded. "There has to be. The DNA tests comparing Emma's gene profile to that of the person whose blood was found on Christina could only come from an identical twin."

"So where is this twin? And why haven't we noticed her walking around town, looking exactly like the Stover girl?" Lily Mae demanded, a triumphant gleam in her eyes.

That was the question the newspaper articles had asked over and over. No one had an answer. The fact that a woman had been present sometime shortly before or during Christina's ordeal didn't prove the woman had killed her. That was why the police had gone ahead and arrested Gavin on circumstantial evidence.

"You're an attorney," Lily Mae continued. "What's your take on the situation?"

"The evidence against Dr. Nighthawk is strong," Hope admitted. "He had opportunity. He certainly had motive."

"Christina was foolish to meet him in the woods," Lily Mae asserted. "When she confronted him with her pregnancy, he probably lost his head. Maybe she demanded marriage or a lot of money so she could leave town. She knew her father would kill her—"

Hope smiled grimly when Lily Mae broke off, realizing where her runaway tongue was taking her.

"Another suspect?" Hope suggested. "Her father found out she was pregnant and, in a fury, hit her, causing her death? He then took the body to the woods and dumped it?"

"But she wasn't dead," Meg said, taking up Hope's scenario. "Gavin found her and delivered the baby, took it to Lettie Brownbear, then returned. But Christina had encountered someone else, fought with him, or *her,* and been killed by having a rock bashed through her skull, according to reports leaked to the newspaper. How gruesome," she said with a shudder.

"Ellis Montgomery would have been furious and upset, but he wouldn't have hurt his youngest child," Winona said. "But neither would Gavin Nighthawk kill anyone. He's taking the blame for someone else."

"Tangled webs," Hope murmured. "This is one of the most complicated cases I've ever seen. We'll have to wait and see what additional evidence is revealed in court."

While her own life seemed mixed up beyond resolution, at least no one had murdered anyone. Yet.

She forced down her qualms about the upcoming hearing on her father's suit. She and Kurt would be facing off with Ross Garrison who was getting advice from Elizabeth Gardener. Gardener had also been hired by Garrett Kincaid to defend Gavin Nighthawk at the urging of Summer Kincaid, Collin's cousin.

Hope didn't know why the famous criminal attorney had actually taken the small-town doctor's case, but chalked it up to the Kincaid powers of persuasion.

Thinking of Saturday and how she'd gone off alone with Collin, she worried that she had allowed herself to be seduced by that same charm—not to mention the sizzling passion between them—and the seeming sincerity of Collin's words and manner.

The psychic, seated to the left of Hope, suddenly reached over and laid her hand lightly on Hope's arm. Hope started, then moved her arm.

"Wait," Winona requested. She closed her eyes and touched Hope again.

"She's getting something," Lily Mae said sotto voce, very seriously. "Be still."

The hairs rose on Hope's neck, but she didn't move. Meg and Lily Mae watched Winona with varying expressions of curiosity and interest. Hope studied the psychic with something akin to fear stirring inside her.

"Take nothing at face value," Winona said just then, as if confirming Hope should be worried about the situation between her and Collin.

"I don't—"

Winona opened her eyes and looked directly at

Hope. "Believe half of what you see and nothing of what you hear," she said, breaking into Hope's reply.

Hope's heart began a loud, insistent pounding. "What do you mean?"

Winona shook her head. "I don't know. I only know that's a message for you. You'll have to interpret it according to what is happening in your life."

"It's something to do with the Baxter lawsuit against the Kincaids," Lily Mae said, butting in with her own interpretation of the psychic's message.

"Maybe." Winona gazed thoughtfully at Hope. "No, I think it's personal. Or maybe both."

Everyone knew of the lawsuit, but Hope wondered if Winona knew she was personally involved with Collin. She sighed. There was no use dwelling on the situation. It only made her head hurt and her heart ache.

"Follow your heart," Meg said suddenly. "I'm trying to get Jordan to listen to his."

"Any success?" Hope asked, and couldn't help the cynical doubt from coming through.

Meg's eyes were kind. "I hope so." She suddenly laughed. "Don't worry about me. I'm a lot tougher than your father. When I get through with him, he won't know whether he's coming or going."

Amazed, Hope could only stare while Lily Mae and Winona laughed uproariously at the outrageous statement.

After the luncheon, Hope returned to her office with the psychic's advice playing over and over in her mind.

Take nothing at face value. Believe half of what you see and nothing of what you hear.

What did those words mean to her?

Nothing, Hope concluded at seven that evening while she stretched her weary back. They were old clichés, easy to dispense as if they had deep meaning. That was the ploy fortune-tellers used on clients, who then applied the sayings to their own lives as though the psychic were astute.

Leaving her office, she headed for the ladies' room before returning to burn the midnight oil. She had a lot of work to do before she left for the evening.

Passing by Kurt's door, which was ajar, she wondered if she should have accepted his offer of dinner. She needed a distraction. She'd been restless and unable to sleep well since Saturday.

Heat spread through her in torrid waves as she recalled the interlude with Collin. And that Kurt had seen them upon their return to town. Apparently he hadn't told her father. At any rate, Jordan hadn't berated her for seeing Collin again, so she assumed he didn't know.

A few steps past Kurt's door, she came to a halt, her heart pounding. She listened intently. Nothing.

Odd, but she thought she'd heard Collin's voice in the other attorney's office. Hearing nothing else, she walked on, blaming her overactive imagination. She returned to her tasks.

At nine Kurt stopped by and told her good-night. "You're working too hard," he scolded, his expression concerned.

"I'll be finished soon. See you in the morning." She smiled until he withdrew, then leaned back in the chair and, swiveling, observed the night sky.

The wind was blowing from the south, bringing clouds from the Beartooth Pass. She felt the loneliness of winter creeping across the land. And into her heart.

At midnight, she locked her desk and hurried out of the office. Taking the steps rather than the elevator to the ground floor, she thought of the odd incident earlier when she'd thought she'd heard Collin's voice inside Kurt's office. She stopped on the second floor.

Believe half of what you see and nothing of what you hear.

What did that mean to her? There was only one point of controversy in her life involving aural evidence—the tape her father had played of Collin and his grandfather planning their strategy on the lawsuit and using her in their plans.

Thoughtfully, she retraced her steps. Going to her father's office, she unlocked it and went inside. A minute later, master keys in hand, she opened the door to Kurt's office. Going in, she closed the door behind her and flipped on the light. The cleaning service wouldn't disturb anyone working late.

She briefly examined the desk and credenza. No, not there. An elaborate bookcase was built along one side of the room. She tried keys she found in the desk until the locked cabinet door of the bookcase opened.

Inside she found an expensive tape-to-tape system. Tapes were filed neatly beneath it. She turned the unit on, read through the tapes and played parts of several. Reviewing the titles again, she frowned in frustration. Apparently she was wrong in the suspicion she'd entertained about Kurt.

She started to close the cabinet. One tape labeled Christmas Party caught her eye. Kurt Peters was not what she would call a sentimental person. Why would he make, much less keep, a tape of the company Christmas feast?

What if it was a tape of another party, a private orgy from the holidays?

Feeling only slightly foolish and guilty for intruding into what might be embarrassing situations, she put in the tape and pressed the Play button.

Collin's voice came eerily through the speakers. His grandfather answered a question, then asked one. They discussed the roundup at the Elk Springs ranch, then the happenings with the family members in Whitehorn.

The tape was three hours long. She listened to every word of illegally taped conversation between Collin and his grandfather. She realized one or the other of the two men was speaking from a cell phone each time.

Looking at the equipment secreted behind the cabinet door, she realized one of the pieces was a radio receiver, the kind people used to listen in on police calls. She also recognized the conversations that had been used to piece together the tape her father had played for her.

None of the conversations referred to her, except one regarding a change of venue in the lawsuit. Just as Collin had said.

Her father had lied.

She had trusted him all her life, believed every word he'd told her. And he had lied.

She had denied the man who loved her in favor of her father. And he had lied.

Ice encased her heart as, her hands trembling, she removed the tape and put it in her briefcase. After locking up, she checked her watch.

It was almost four in the morning. She had time for a shower and meal, time to compose her questions, before meeting with her father in his office at seven. She would invite Kurt to the meeting.

No. She wanted to see her father alone. And there was only one question, really.

"Jordan is ready to see you," her father's secretary informed her at two minutes after seven.

"Thank you."

Hope hung up the phone and picked up her briefcase. She walked down the hall and entered the CEO's outer office.

"Would you like some coffee?" the secretary asked, giving her a welcoming smile.

"No, thanks." In the past three hours she'd had enough caffeine to keep her awake for a week. "Good morning, Father," she said upon entering his office. She made sure the door closed completely behind her.

He nodded to her, finished reading a report and laid the paper on his desk. "You were in early this morning," he said, approval in his voice and smile.

"Yes." She removed a portable tape player from the briefcase and placed it on a side table. After plugging it into a wall socket, she turned to him. "I have something you might be interested in."

She'd already set the tape to the sections she was interested in. She pushed the Play button. Collin and his grandfather held their conversation about a birthday present for Collin's sister, a filly Collin was training. They then discussed the price of beef and other ranching interests and hung up.

"Notice that neither my name nor the lawsuit was mentioned once," she said.

She fast-forwarded to another section. During a fifteen-minute conversation of Kincaid affairs, the possible change of venue was mentioned only at the end. Garrett referred to her as the "young lawyer gal" but there was nothing deprecating in his tone. She played a couple of other sections that didn't mention her at all.

"Here's the last one," she said, clicking the tape on when her father stirred restlessly.

"I don't want to see you hurt, boy," Garrett said.

"I'm okay," Collin replied. "I'll be in Whitehorn in another hour. Who's at the ranch this weekend?"

Garrett ignored the change of subject. "If you love that little gal, you'd better go after her."

"She has to come to me. I've told her how I feel."

Hope flinched at the bitterness in his quiet voice. It hurt her someplace deep inside.

"Tell her again," his grandfather urged. "Women get strange notions when left on their own."

"Or when they're lied to by the person they trust above all others," Hope said into the silence at the end of the recorded conversation. She looked at her father. "Why?"

He sighed and ran a hand through his hair. "It was for your own good, bumpkins. I saw you falling under the Kincaid spell. I couldn't let you be taken in that way."

Fury shook her from her head to her toes. "You wanted me taken in by you, by your lies. I should turn you and your faithful partner-in-crime over to the district attorney."

Her father had the grace to blush. "Leave Kurt out of this. He did me a favor by recording those conversations."

"They were all innocent. He doctored the tape to make it sound as if they planned to use me. Did you know that when you played it to me?"

"Not then," he admitted. "Later I figured it out."

"But you didn't bother to tell me."

She packed up the tape, retrieved the doctored one and put them both in her briefcase. She headed for the door.

"Where are you going?" her father asked warily.

"To Collin. I'm going to ask his forgiveness for doubting him. On my knees, if necessary. Then, if he loves me as much as I love him, I'm going to ask him to marry me. I want children, Father, *his* children, and a life with him. If he'll have me."

Jordan flushed a dangerous red. "You go to him and you're out of here. No position. No inheritance. Nothing."

She gave him a pitying glance as she opened the door. "There's nothing for me here. There may be nothing for me at the Kincaid ranch, either, but I'm going there to see." She gestured to the briefcase. "I won't give these to Collin to use against you, but don't expect anything else from me. Not ever." She hesitated. "Goodbye, Father."

He didn't answer.

The secretary kept her eyes on her desk as Hope left. At her office, she picked up her purse and a box of personal items. She told a wide-eyed Selma goodbye and walked out.

In the car, driving toward the Kincaid ranch, she felt no freedom, only a sense of loss so profound, it reached all the way to her soul. It was hard to leave a child's love and faith behind, but she had to.

When she stopped at the horse rail on the Kincaid

spread, she wondered if Collin was there. She didn't think she could bear it if he wasn't. She needed him desperately.

She turned off the engine and climbed out. A tall male walked out of the house. He had dark hair, but the sun was so bright in her face while his was in shadow that she couldn't tell who it was.

"Collin?"

"I'm coming," he said.

Tears blinded her. She opened her arms. In three seconds she was safe in his. "I've come...I've come..." That was all she could get out.

"Shh," he murmured. "It's enough that you're here. We can talk later." He held her tenderly. "My heart," he whispered into her hair. "My soul."

Thirteen

"Time to rise and shine," a soft baritone whispered. "I know you're awake."

Hope opened her eyes as Collin slid his hands under her and lifted her into his arms. "Mmm," she said, not wanting to stir. Last night she'd been exhausted when they went to bed, considering her sleepless previous night and the morning's confrontation with her father.

Collin had taken her to his room, although he'd offered her one of her own. "I want to be with you," she'd told him.

In his bed, he had simply held her. She'd gone to sleep, her arms around him, his warmth, his sweet tenderness easing the tears that filled her heart.

Yesterday they had strolled hand in hand around

the ranch, sometimes talking but mostly just being together. The Kincaid brothers and their wives had left them alone. She'd been grateful.

Collin had been sympathetic to her loss of faith in her father. It was only after she had talked out her grief to him that she realized he'd gone through the same loss with his father, but at a much earlier age. Her heart had ached anew, this time for the boy.

"I had my grandfather," he'd told her. "He was my salvation, the North Star that guided me."

Once her father had been that for her. She pressed her face against his throat as the tears, which refused to fall, burned against her eyes.

"It'll work out," he promised again, the light of the new day effecting a halo around his head. "Do you think you can eat some breakfast? I've got it ready."

"Yes. Let me up so I can shower and dress."

He chuckled and hugged her close for a second. "I like you best this way."

"Men," she retorted, forcing the cheer.

She pulled his T-shirt over her head and rushed to the shower. In less than fifteen minutes she was ready, dressed in the slacks and white blouse she'd worn the previous day.

Collin had waited. Together they walked to the dining room. His grandfather was there.

"Good morning," he said, kindness in his eyes. "I found breakfast ready and helped myself. I hope that was okay."

Collin greeted the older man. "I made enough for everyone."

Hope ate the scrambled eggs, bacon and English muffins Collin had prepared. As the two men talked ranching business, she was glad just to listen and not be expected to take part.

Studying Collin and Garrett, she realized they had the same muscular build, the same smile with the crinkles at the corners of their eyes and the same way of slightly tilting their heads as they considered a question.

When he was Garrett's age, Collin would look very much like his relative. He would probably have his grandfather's temper, but he would also have his gentleness and his concern for his children's and grandchildren's welfare.

Through the darkness of worry and sadness inside her came a single guiding ray of light. This man was her future. Her love. And she was his. She had been right to come to him.

Unable to contain herself, Hope touched his arm, once, quickly, but with feeling.

Collin paused in what he was saying and looked at the woman who had come to him so unexpectedly. Manna from heaven, he'd thought, observing her exhausted sleep before waking her this morning. He'd hated to disturb her, feeling that sleep might help heal her spirit, but he'd wanted this time alone with her and his grandfather.

His heart lurched at what he saw in her eyes. "Shall we tell Granddad we're going to be married as soon as possible?" he asked softly.

She nodded. No protest. No postponement. No hesitation. Just a simple nod of agreement. Relief poured through him like sunshine on water, sending long warming rays down to the rock bottom of his soul. He realized that some part of him had thought they would never be together, that Jordan in his hatred of his family would somehow keep Hope from him.

When he glanced at his grandfather, his heart lurched again. The old man had tears in his eyes. Collin felt choked up himself.

"Congratulations, son," Garrett said in a husky tone. "You've got yourself a keeper in this little lawyer gal."

"I agree." He lifted Hope's hand and planted a kiss on the back. "We'll have to shop for a ring today." He paused. "Your father will hear of it."

"We should call Lily Mae and let her get the word out before we go to town," Hope suggested wryly. "That way, maybe no one will faint at the sight of a Baxter and a Kincaid together."

He loved her for many reasons, but right now he loved her most for her spunk. She had courage, this woman. He tempered his happiness at having her to himself, respectful of the grief she tried so hard to conceal.

"You'll never be sorry that you came to me," he murmured. "We'll have a good life."

"I know."

She smiled at him, her gaze sweet and lambent and adoring. His heart grew too large for his chest.

"Good morning," Gina said, coming in and heading straight for the coffeepot. "Mmm, this is good and just what I need. I've been up since five."

"Why so early?" Garrett asked.

She grinned, kissed him on the cheek and took her place at the table. "I've found your other grandson."

There was an electrified silence.

"Who? Where? Are you sure?" Garrett asked in rapid succession, excitement adding color to his lean cheeks.

"Yes. I narrowed it down to two births on the same day. One was a girl. The other was a boy. From your son's notes, the baby he believed was his was a boy."

Garrett nodded. "According to his datebook/journal, Larry found out a former flame had given birth to a baby boy and he suspected the child was his because of the timing. Who is it? Do you have a name?" Garrett demanded, displaying the family trait of controlled impatience.

Gina glanced at Hope, then back at Garrett. "Meg Reilly. Her son Gabe is Larry Kincaid's last child."

"No," Hope said, shocked. "It can't be Meg. She…"

Hope let the rest of the thought fade. It could be Meg. She'd admitted she'd wanted only a baby from the man, nothing else. Larry Kincaid had apparently taken his pleasure wherever it was offered with no thought of tomorrow or the possible consequences, let alone that he might have been used.

"Seven sons," Garrett said. "Eight," he corrected, looking apologetically at Collin, who was the only legitimate one.

Collin shrugged. "Mom divorced him because of his womanizing. It was no secret to me. Although seven brothers was a bit of a surprise."

"What are you going to do about Meg and Gabe?" Hope asked, concern for her friend overcoming her own problems as she waited for Garrett to answer.

"I want the boy to have his rightful inheritance," Garrett told them, "the same as his brothers. And I want to have a place in all my grandsons's lives." His expression softened. "I would never try to take the child from his mother. That would be wrong."

Hope laid her fork down. "Would you mind if I go to her and ask if it's true?" She glanced apologetically at Gina. "Only Meg can really tell us. Unless you plan to demand DNA testing?"

"I'd rather not go that far," Garrett said.

Hope was relieved.

Gina was thoughtful. "I've met Meg. She's an honest person. She'll tell the truth when asked."

"We'll go to town as soon as we finish," Collin promised. He gave her a worried glance. "I wonder how your father is going to take this news."

Hope gasped. "Gabe! He's—he's a Kincaid!"

"Right."

"My father will have a stroke," she declared grimly, her concern for Meg increasing.

Garrett broke the stark silence with a chuckle. "It's the final irony—or outrage, however one might want to view it."

Gina hid a smile behind her hand, then joined in the laughter. Hope couldn't help it; she laughed, too, a bit hysterically, but it was funny. Larry Kincaid had gotten the last laugh on all of them.

Collin added his deep chuckle.

"What's so funny?" Trent asked, entering the dining room with his son in his arms.

The other four laughed all that much harder.

"Oh, no," Hope said when Collin parked in Meg's driveway. Her earlier laughter at the situation was gone. Worry had taken its place. "That's my father's car."

"Do you want to come back another time?"

She quelled the tremor that pulsed through her. "No. The news is going to come out. He may as well hear it before anyone else."

"Maybe you'd better let Meg tell him."

"I will. I'll talk to her privately. Do you think—"

"Your father and I can stay in the same room without coming to blows?" he finished for her. "I'll make a point of being on my best behavior. After all, I got you out of the deal." He kissed her gently.

Feeling buoyed by his support, Hope led the way

to the cottage door. She rang the bell. It opened almost at once.

"Why, hello," Meg said, surprise darting across her face as she stared at her two visitors.

"May we come in?" Hope asked.

"Your father is here," Meg warned.

"I know, but I have to talk to you."

Meg's green eyes darkened. Hope thought she saw fear flicker in them for a second, then Meg nodded.

"I think I know what this is about. Jordan may as well hear it, too."

Hope touched her friend's arm briefly in sympathy. "Are you sure?"

Meg's smile was resigned to the fate she knew was coming. Hope realized her friend had been expecting this.

"Hope and Collin are here," Meg said.

Jordan was seated at the pine table. Gabe was in his high chair, stuffing cereal into his mouth. "Hop," he crowed in delight upon seeing her.

Hope gave him a kiss and a tickle, then directed the child back to his breakfast. She finally looked at her father. "Hello," she said.

His face reddened with anger, but he nodded.

"This is about Gabe," Hope told Meg, wanting to make sure the other woman understood her secret was out.

"I was sure it was. Sit down, you two," Meg invited. She poured them each a cup of coffee.

"This may be a long discussion." She turned to Jordan. "You are to listen. I don't want any first-reaction comments."

Puzzled, he hesitated, then nodded.

"Promise," Meg insisted.

"All right. I promise," Jordan added when she continued to look sternly at him.

She took a breath. "Larry Kincaid fathered Gabe." She looked across the table and smiled slightly at Hope. "That was your news, wasn't it?"

In the silence that followed, Hope felt Collin take her hand and squeeze it. "Yes. Gina discovered the birth records and told us this morning."

Meg sighed. "I knew it was a matter of time. I've been worrying about it, wondering what I should do…what would be best for Gabe. I don't want him hurt or confused by a custody battle. If it comes to that. I won't give my son up. You can tell your grandfather—"

"I have enough money," Jordan said, giving Collin a challenging glare. "We can fight him on equal terms."

"There won't be a custody battle," Collin said, speaking to Meg and ignoring Jordan. "My grandfather would never try to take your child from you. He would like a place in Gabe's life, though. Also, Gabe will be included in the inheritance my grandfather is providing for his other grandsons. Whatever it turns out to be," he added with a challenging glare of his own directed at Jordan.

"That's generous," Meg said slowly. "I'll have to talk to him and find out his expectations. I knew in my heart, if I stayed here in Whitehorn, I would have to face this. It's probably best it came out now."

Jordan snorted. "Don't be taken in by the Kincaid charm," he warned. "They smile out of one side of their mouths and lie out of the others. They'll turn your own son against you if you don't watch out."

Meg rounded on him. "That's enough," she said firmly.

Gabe quit eating and glanced at the adults in his young life. Hope smiled reassuringly and patted his shoulder. He gave her a milky grin. It disappeared when he looked at his mother then Jordan.

"The Kincaids—Garrett and Collin—have been fair with you," Meg said to her lover, her gaze locked on his. "You have to let go of this obsession you have for revenge."

Jordan's face might have been comical with shock had the situation not been so serious. Hope couldn't bear to look at her father, to witness his humiliation as Meg turned on him.

"So you're going over to their side, too?" he said on a quieter note.

"The way your daughter did?" Meg shot back at him. "You've lost her. Are you going to lose me and Gabe, too? The Kincaids don't have to destroy you. You're doing a damn good job on your own."

Jordan's eyes went as cold and flat as steel rivets. Hope had seen the expression many times. Collin squeezed her hand again, warning her to not interfere.

Meg pushed a hand into her hair. Her fingers were trembling. "When you came to me last night and said Hope had gone to Collin, I prayed that you would stop this senseless revenge. I thought her leaving would make you see reason. This morning, when you said you were disowning your own flesh and blood, I realized it was hopeless."

"Please don't worry about me," Hope told her friend. "If your happiness lies with my father, don't throw it away."

"I had already decided to tell him not to come back," Meg said sadly. She turned to Jordan. "I can't take a chance on your hurting Gabe because he was sired by a Kincaid."

"Hope is an adult. She chose to go to our enemy. Gabe is a baby. His parentage is hardly his fault," Jordan said stiffly.

"But it's mine. I didn't know Larry's real name at the time, but it wouldn't have mattered if I had. I discovered who he was when he was killed and his picture appeared on television and in all the papers."

"He deceived you and yet you defend the Kincaids?" Jordan asked incredulously.

She shrugged. "It was mutual opportunism. He wanted a night's fling without complications. I wanted a child. Simple. Only life never is, is it?"

She touched Jordan's cheek in a tender caress that smote Hope's heart at the hopelessness in it.

"If we married," Meg said, "then someday, when we're having a quarrel as all couples do at some point, you'll bring Larry Kincaid up. You'll say cruel things about me and my son's father and about Gabe's conception. Words like that can never be erased once they're spoken. I won't allow Gabe to be hurt by your obsession for revenge the way you've hurt your daughter."

"So you're cutting me out of your life, just like that." Jordan snapped his fingers.

"No, with a lot of heartache and anguish," she corrected softly. "I love you. In many ways, you're a wonderful person…" She sighed and shook her head. "But you won't be a whole person until you give up your hatred. It's hard to give up a boyhood dream, Jordan, but you're a man. Let it go," she pleaded softly.

Hope watched her father and her best friend as they sat immobile, staring at each other. Please, she prayed, please let it be all right. Make him see, please make him see.

But it wasn't to be.

Jordan stood. "You've made your choice," he told Meg. Without another glance at any of them, he walked out.

The silence stretched for several seconds. "Well," Meg said shakily. "Well."

Tears filled her eyes. Seeing them, Gabe clouded up and let out a wail, not understanding what was wrong but knowing his world was terribly off balance at the moment.

Hope took the toddler into her arms. "I'm so sorry, Meg," she said. "I'm so very sorry."

"It isn't your fault. I knew the situation. I took the risk. Win some, lose some," she said. "When should I call your grandfather?" she asked Collin.

"He's at the ranch. He'll be delighted to hear from you at any time."

She made the call and was smiling when she hung up. "Your grandfather is a gentle man," she said. "I'm glad Gabe is going to have him."

"There's none better," Collin assured her. He looked at Hope. "Do you want to pick up some clothes at your place?"

She nodded. "All of them. I want to sell the condo. It was never a home."

"Don't grieve too much," Meg whispered when they hugged each other upon saying farewell. "He made his choice. Let him live with it."

"I know. I will," she promised. "There's nothing else to do. But he's going to be terribly lonely."

"Yes," Meg agreed. "Maybe some good will come of it."

They tried to smile and ended comforting each other while they dried their tears. If nothing else, Hope knew she and Meg had come through this the best of friends.

In the pickup driving back to the ranch, Collin gave her a sympathetic perusal. "Grandchildren often bridge the distance between the parents and grandparents," he told her.

"Not my father," she said. "He'll never forgive me for choosing a Kincaid over him. There's no going back."

He took her hand. "I'll be here. Always. That's a promise."

She knew he would keep it.

Jordan slammed the door behind him. He stalked down the hall from the three-car garage to the study. After pouring a drink, he tossed it back in one burning gulp, then grimaced in distaste and set the glass aside. Alcohol had never solved any problem, he'd observed as a young man, watching his uncle try to drown his troubles.

He let his gaze run over the room. Once, the expensive furnishings and tasteful arrangements had been a deep source of pride and comfort to him. They offered nothing now. This was just an empty room that echoed every sound. Except for the distant hum of the air-conditioning, the house was totally silent. It closed around him like a tomb. With one swipe of his hand he swept the array of fine crystal off the gleaming antique sideboard, sending it to the floor when it shattered with a satisfying racket. Then all was silent again.

When he cursed, his voice echoed eerily back at him.

Sitting in his chair, he stared out the window at the view of the town highlighted in the glaring brightness of the day. He felt smothered by the filtered air coming from the vent, and his chest hurt with each breath. Vaguely he wondered if he could be having a heart attack.

If he did, no one would know until the maid came in later to dust and straighten the house. There was no one to call. His daughter was gone. Meg had thrown him out.

Kurt would come, but Jordan didn't want him. The man was good at his job, but he wasn't the son Jordan had secretly wanted. Kurt hadn't a tenth the integrity that Hope had.

Jordan closed his eyes as a shudder went through him. He had never thought she would leave. What had happened to the little girl who had adored him?

She grew up, some painfully honest part of him answered.

She fell for a Kincaid, he scoffed.

He fell for her, too. You could have had Meg. And Gabe. You chose the loneliness.

He was shocked at the admission. Of course he'd walked away from that absurd ultimatum. Women. What did they know of business and justice? They thought with their hearts.

Yes.

The word echoed through his heart. His empty heart. He thought of Hope, of Meg, of Gabe and his glad smile, his demands for "Jor" to carry him.

Something hard landed in the middle of his chest. It rose to his throat, choking him, smothering him, crumpling all the walls he'd worked for years to build. A sound, harsh and violent, echoed in the eerie silence, then another.

For the first time in his life Jordan Baxter wept for all the things he'd lost, for the boy who had wanted too much, for the man who'd sought revenge, who'd made money and gained a foothold in the world... and had nothing.

It was a hard, cold truth. He'd truly lost everything.

An hour later, showered and changed, he backed out of the drive of the empty mansion. He had a trip to make, a long one, but he would do it.

First he had to see his attorney and tell her he'd decided to accept the Kincaid offer. Then he had to see a certain wedding planner to see if he could schedule a wedding. A big one. He would have to invite all his enemies. The Kincaids outnumbered him about twenty to one. He grimaced at the sheer audacity of his plans.

But then, that was how he'd made his fortune.

"Someone's here," Gina said, her face solemn when she stepped aside.

Hope looked up from the carpet where she played patty-cake with Gabe according to his rules. Collin was also on the floor beside them. He had already done peek-a-boo with his new half brother until Gabe had decided it was Hope's turn to entertain him. Meg and Garrett, Trent, Brandon and Emma completed their group.

A pain speared right down into her heart when she saw her father. Collin and Garrett got to their feet and moved in front until they stood shoulder to shoulder, a phalanx to guard those they held dear.

Jordan held up his hands, palms out. "Put away your weapons. I come in peace." He glanced past the two men. "I need to speak to my attorney."

Confused, Hope rose. She wasn't his attorney anymore, but he was looking at her. She smoothed her shirt, then stepped forward. Collin dropped an arm around her shoulder and watched Jordan warily.

"Yes?" she said, sounding very much like her legal persona.

"I've decided to accept the latest Kincaid offer," he said.

She thought her hearing must be off. It sounded as if he'd said he wanted to settle. "You accept?"

Meg jumped to her feet. "Jordan," she said on a choked breath, as if he'd just offered her the moon.

"I was coming to see you next," he told her. "How big a wedding do you want?" He glanced around the room. "There's a damn lot of Kincaids. I suppose we'd better invite them all or else this feud will continue forever."

The next thing Hope knew Meg had made a giant leap and thrown herself at her father. He was holding on to her best friend as if he'd never let her go.

"Am I seeing things?" she asked Collin in wonder.

"We're hallucinating together," he assured her, a wry smile settling on his mouth. "Looks like we're going to be one big happy family after all."

Jordan hugged Meg to his side, then held an arm out to Hope. "You have my blessing. Will you give me yours?"

"Of course," she said, still feeling dazed. She took the necessary step and was enclosed in a bear hug. Tears stung her eyes. It was like coming home again.

"I love you, bumpkins," he whispered into her hair.

"Love you, too," she murmured.

"Welcome home, sir," Collin said, holding out his hand as if welcoming Jordan back from a long, grueling trip.

The two men shook hands. Jordan did the same with Garrett, then each of the other Kincaids.

"Why?" Meg demanded. "How—"

"It was that damned big house," he said. "That big empty house. It needs a passel of kids and grandkids to fill it up."

"Ah-hh," she said in understanding.

"Jor," Gabe shouted, as if wanting his share of this wonderful laughter and strange goings-on of the adults.

Jordan swung him up into his arms. "How would you like to change that to Daddy?" he asked, and was relieved to see the smiles on Meg's and Hope's faces.

"You're quiet," Collin said.

"I'm still in shock," Hope explained.

They walked hand in hand among the cottonwoods along the creek that ran through the meadow. Horses and cows grazed or dozed in the surrounding pastures while the sun set with a last fiery toss of color across the sky.

"It had to work out," he said reasonably. "I love you too much to have you unhappy about anything in your life."

She reached up on tiptoe and kissed his chin. "Your grandfather was so gracious. He'll be a wonderful influence on our children."

"Hey, I'm going to be a wonderful influence."

She laughed, then sighed. "I know. I'm so happy right now, I'm afraid I'm going to wake up."

He leaned against a cottonwood which shimmered with the brilliant red-gold leaves that heralded fall and the dormant season beyond that, and pulled her close against him.

"Never," he whispered. "This is one dream that's going to last, this one we share." He bent to her mouth.

He kissed her then. She felt all the promises of life rush into her heart and soul. Eagerly she reached out for them, giving him kiss for kiss.

"Beloved enemy," he said when they came up for air, his gaze overwhelming her with his tenderness.

"Life is settling down, isn't it?" she asked philosophically. "Us falling in love. My father in love and marrying Meg, adopting a Kincaid. The lawsuit dropped. I think the Baxter and Kincaid feud has finally been put to rest."

She felt his smile as his lips moved against her temple. "Yes," he agreed.

Playfully she poked him in the ribs. "Don't get to thinking the Kincaids won," she warned.

"I won. I got you. That's all I care about." He tucked her under his arm and headed back toward the house.

She sighed contentedly, feeling loved as she never had. For herself. For simply existing.

Life. It wasn't so complicated, after all.

* * * * *

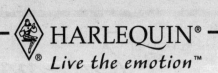

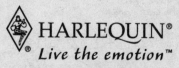

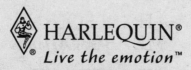

HARLEQUIN®
INTRIGUE®

BREATHTAKING ROMANTIC SUSPENSE

Shared dangers and passions lead to electrifying
romance and heart-stopping suspense!

Every month, you'll meet six new heroes
who are guaranteed to make your spine tingle
and your pulse pound. With them you'll enter
into the exciting world of Harlequin Intrigue—
where your life is on the line
and so is your heart!

THAT'S INTRIGUE—
ROMANTIC SUSPENSE
AT ITS BEST!

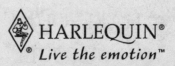

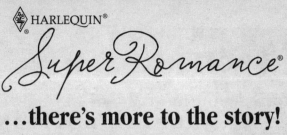
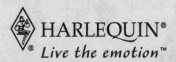